Rustrocket

Tales of the fiercely independent motorcycle club

By A.T.Cross

You should start out knowing that most of this is bullshit. Don't go reading too far into it. If by some chance, you think you see somebody that resembles you in it, relax, it's only your shadow. Just enjoy the ride. Oh, and don't try this at home. I'm a trained professional.

In most books, this is where they put a lot of fine print. unless you want to write an article about me, or quote me on Facebook, or whatever. I actually stole that shit from another book. Other things I stole? Macramé is derived from the Arabic word "Migramah" believed to mean "embroidered veil" Sailors made macramé objects in off-hours while at sea, and sold or bartered them when they landed... spreading the art to the new world....It was long crafted by sailors, especially in elaborate or ornamental knotting forms, to decorate anything from knife handles to bottles, to parts of ships...(Thank-you Sarah.) No animals were harmed in the writing of this book, unless you count the hundreds of bugs in my garage and basement who suffered irreversible lung damage from the amount of second hand smoke that they inhaled. This entire book is composed of 100% recycled cruelty free vegan plotlines stolen from other people's entirely legitimate books. Well, there goes any semblance of professionalism. Ah hell oh well. Hi Mom!

Please feel free to paw through the rusted out scrapheap of my website:
www.Rustrocket.com

ISBN: 1453880720
ISBN-13: 978-1453880722

For all my friends,

(N.D.Y.)

"The mind is its own place and in itself,
can make a Heaven of Hell, a Hell of Heaven."

-- John Milton

Prologue: A room without walls

The clouds hung low over the city, more lavender than grey, swirling around the buildings, leaving the streets wet and glistening. The rain descended, moving silently down the alley to pool at my feet. It wasn't a weather pattern, so much as atmosphere, already soaking into my jacket, dripping down the back of my neck. It was an appropriate sort of miserable.

I sat outside Randy's bar, smoking another cigarette, and staring up the alley toward the radio towers on top of Capitol Hill. I didn't know what time it was, but the doors were closed, and inside the bar, the last few bodies moved around, dim silhouettes in a candle lit procession. Half way through the second cigarette, the door swung open. Randy leaned out, glanced up the alley, and glanced back at me.

"I told you not to do it," he said.

I shrugged.

"Well come in," he said.

Picking up my saddlebags, I leaned forward, and shuffled toward the door.

"What's that?" he asked.

"What's left of my life."

"Well come in already." He held the door for me. "She left then?"

"Gone and gone." I shrugged. "Now I'm homeless."

He shook his head and followed me into the bar. Lue and Jordan watched me as I dragged in.

"Hello, Cap'n!" Jordan grinned.

"You didn't do it," Lue said.

Randy must have nodded his head, because Lue shook hers. "We told you it was a bad idea."

I shrugged.

"How many did you take?"

"All of them."

"Oh no," she said.

I nodded.

"What were you thinking?"

"I wasn't."

"You're surprisingly lucid," Jordan said.

"Medicine only works if you need it." I dropped the saddlebags beside a stool and took a seat. "Otherwise it just fucks us hard."

Randy took his place behind the bar, folded his arms across his chest, and sort of smiled a glare.

"Please?" I asked.

He glanced away, pulled the bottle of Jim Beam from the rack, and poured me out a binge-ender shot.

"Could I get a Manny's chaser?"

He glanced back at the taps, pulled a bucket glass from the rack, and filled it. "So, what next?"

I shook my head. "I don't know."

"Where are you going to go?"

I sipped my whiskey. "I'm homeless now."

Jordan slapped my back. "You aren't homeless." It was pretty clear that she'd been drinking too long.

"Well, I have no home."

"So what's new?" Lue laughed.

"You can stay on the couch at the Compound," Randy said.

I hunkered down over my bourbon.

"Provided that you don't ruin any more of our clocks," Lue said.

Jordan nodded her agreement.

I took a sip and sputtered.

Jordan took pity and squeezed my shoulder. Lue frowned for me.

"It's like a limb," Randy said. "You got to cut it off and forget about it."

Lue raised an eyebrow at him. "Oh yeah?"

He grabbed a towel and wiped at the bar. "Just cut it off," he said.

I nodded.

"Alright, you ready?" Jordan glanced over at Lue.

"Let's go," Lue said.

“See you guys soon,” Jordan said. Randy nodded. I nodded. They collected their things and strolled out.

Randy poured himself a kicker of Roger’s, flipped off most of the lights, and dragged his keys across the bar. He took a seat next to me.

“I warned you,” he said.

I nodded.

“But you did it anyway.”

“Whoop.” I smiled. “Whoop whoop.”

He smiled and took a sip. “Good to see you, Cap’n.”

I shrugged again. “Yeah, Conduit, I didn’t want it to end like this.”

“Too late now, huh?”

“Too high for this shit.”

He took another sip, shrugged, and set his little glass of beer on the bar. “Life is what happens while we’re making other plans.”

“How trite.”

“Fine, fucker.” He downed the rest of his beer and nodded at my drinks. “Finish those. We’ll get some crispitos on the way home.”

“I have no home now.”

He smiled, picked up his keys, and waited for me to down my drinks and collect my saddlebags. “You’ll always have a home, Cap’n.”

Church is in session

"Aaron," she whispered in my ear.

I woke up face down on the carpet, my sleeping bag kicked a few feet away. The blinds were shut and my alarm clock was buried under piles of laundry. "Habibi?" The condo was empty. I was losing track of time entirely. My beard itched.

I got up to take a leak and found her last love letters scrawled across the bathroom mirror in a purple Crayola marker. "I love you. I'll miss you," she wrote. "*Nothing*, so much *nothing*." And of course, "(.)" Her pink loofah still hung from the bathtub faucet. There were a half-dozen bobby pins on the edge of the sink. I felt like a stalker. Anything to prove that she existed, that I didn't dream her this time.

I ran some water over my head and inspected my face in the mirror. I am a man who has no business trying to grow a beard. My sideburns pushed their borders out into a sparse savannah of hair on my cheek and little more on my chin or lip. Maybe Arabic men could grow a beard when their lover was gone, but I got scruffy. I brushed my teeth and spread lotion over the fresh ink scabs on my back.

Mat didn't do as much tattoo work as he used to. He'd been focusing on his chopper business. I was in the chair the day he quit his job at the parlor. He quit before noon and spent the next six hours hand-copying Picasso's watercolor of Don Quixote on my left shoulder. He wasn't much of a drinker, but afterward, he let me take him across the street and buy him a cocktail. I figured, a guy quit a place he'd been at since it opened, he was bound to need a drink.

He'd been at that parlor for twelve years. He joked about pulling out everything that was his, including, but not limited to: the flooring, two tattoo chairs, the autoclave, the gazebo out front, various display cases, the bathroom sink. After sitting through that afternoon, I guess I was grandfathered in for ink work.

Post tattoo shop, getting ink done meant sitting in a dentist chair in his cold garage. After he did the crow outline, I asked him about motorcycle parts. Mat recommended a motorcycle salvage yard in Escondido. He said that it wasn't the only one, but that it was probably my best bet. They were in the Yellow Pages and had all the parts I needed.

I showered, dressed, smoked a bowl, and spent an hour wandering the empty condo, kicking at piles of projects that I should work on. When I found myself kicking the piles that I'd already kicked, I left for the salvage shop with a hundred dollars' worth of Mat's tattoo money left in my pocket.

The place was set in a strip of industrial shops and warehouses, auto body shops, mechanic shops, a hotrod place. There were a few parking spots in front of the door. The yard to the left was all bikes in various stages of entropy, caged in chain link. The front door opened into a small sales room, accessories, and such lining shelves and motley display racks. Every square inch of the place seemed to hold motorcycle parts. In the back was a desk set before a garage door. The warehouse had ceiling-high shelves filled with boxes of parts.

The parts guy was greasy and thin, wiping his hands on a rag. It looked like I caught him in the middle of an operation. He wore thick glasses and flipped through a stack of books searching for serial numbers. While he wandered around in the back, I glanced through the shelves of manuals, but I couldn't find one for the EX. He came back with handlebar clips, a handful of turn signals, a new petcock, and a couple of sparkplugs.

"I've got a couple tanks that might work." He looked at the back of his hand for a clean space to wipe his nose. "You want to come back and take a look?"

I followed him into the warehouse. The shelves seemed infinite. He pulled a tall ladder out of the corner, spread it out in an aisle, and carried a long pole with a hook at the end. As he took the first few steps, he paused, adjusted his glasses and squinted upward. A few hundred gas tanks hung from wire coat hangers and a series of cables woven across the ceiling, the last available surface in the place. He picked his target and climbed unsteadily, but like he was used to it at least. He straddled the top of the ladder and stretched the pole toward a blue tank. As he set his hook, the cables shook, rattling the whole web. The tanks rang like churchbells as they banged against each other.

“This one’s pretty clean, a little dent in one side, but not too bad.” He swung the pole toward me, offering me the blue tank. The ringing of the tanks hung in my ears as I took it and wiped the dust off. There were a few flecks of rust inside, but *nothing* like the old tank. I thanked him and collected the armful of parts from the counter on my way to the cash register.

On the way back from Escondido I stopped by my parents’ place to borrow the vacuum and drop off the parts. My nephew and his friend were at the curb, kicking a ball back and forth on the sidewalk. He came screaming and hollering, climbed on the Jeep and begged me to park with him riding the runner.

“What's that?” He pointed in at the passenger seat.

“Parts for the motorcycle.”

“That thing runs?”

“Yes.”

“Nanny said she'd never ride on a duct-taped motorcycle.”

“Nanny doesn't have to.”

“That thing doesn't run.”

“I drove it here.”

“Papa Steve won't let us play on it.”

“He doesn't much want me playing on it either.”

He and his friend tailed me into the garage where I pulled a stack of papers off the seat and tried to prop the rearview mirror back up.

"That thing does not run." He said matter-of-factly.

I opened the garage door and set up the tools.

“I’ll bet you can’t get it running,” he said.

“I’ll bet I can.”

I pushed the key in. I hadn’t charged the battery in a few months, but she turned over on the first shot and muttered to herself, a little shaky on the throttle. I opened the choke so she roared.

The boys laughed and shook their heads. They wanted to ride it on some rampage through the streets, figuring that's how I did it, bouncing off walls and Dumpsters and lampposts until it finally came to rest in the garage. They raced off, twisting imaginary throttles, playing at motorcycle demolition drivers.

I watched them go. “All I need is thirteen-hundred miles, Rosinante.” I petted her windshield, turned the key off, and let her rest. The rearview mirror dropped limp again, angled up into the corner of the garage. I stacked the papers back on her seat.

Flight testing

"Do you believe in fate?" Miguelito asked. He was doing seventy in a forty-five zone, careening down Highway 101 through Carlsbad. His hair was all wild in the wind and his long, braided beard whipped around his chin.

"You ask me that all the time."

"I think we met for a reason." He swerved to pass a little white VW Rabbit and glanced over as we came up on the left side. Two girls looked over from the white Rabbit. Miguelito smiled. He slowed to match their speed. "Say something to them."

"Say what?"

"I don't know, *Guapo*. You're the wordsmith."

I leaned out the window and smiled at the driver of the Rabbit. "Hi," I yelled. "My name is Aaron, and this is Michael. I think he likes you because this is the first time he's taken his foot off the gas since we got into the car."

Michael smiled and nodded.

The driver looked nervous. The other girl leaned forward. "That's not a lane," she yelled back.

I glanced over at Michael. "She's right, you know."

Miguelito leaned forward to check her out. He smiled wider, slammed on the brakes, and slid behind the Rabbit. "I thought you said you were some sort of love poet."

"Look man, you're going to get us arrested," I told him.

"Not yet," he said. He gunned the engine, bounced up onto the sidewalk, and pulled up along the right side of the white Rabbit. "Hi," he said to the girl in the passenger seat.

She scoffed at him. He slammed on the brakes and veered to the left, bouncing off the curb, narrowly missing a parked car, and almost clipping the white Rabbit's back bumper. The girls glanced back nervously. When the left lane opened again he veered around the Rabbit, stomped the accelerator, and sailed past.

"Some love poet," he muttered.

"It's hard to holler love poetry at fifty miles per hour, fucker."

Miguelito pulled in behind the restaurant and nearly fell out of the car. His mother was standing at the back door watching. "*Mi'jo*!" she screamed at him. She's a little Peruvian woman with painted eyebrows. She met Michael's father when he was working for the Peace Corps in Cuzco. "*Ay carajo borracho pendejo*!" she yelled at me. "Why are you taking my son to go drinking?" She has this sort of regal roll to her R that made drinking sound exquisite.

I climbed out of the passenger side. "*Ah Carmenita, besame*." I tried to hug her.

Michael dug in the back seat to find his kitchen shoes.

"You get away from me," she said. "He has to work." She pointed at her son. "And you get him drunk."

"He got me drunk," I explained, but it was no good.

"Ah ma, I'm good." He adjusted his lapels and smoothed his hair back.

"*Ay carajo*," she said again. I used to think that it was my nickname, something like "dearest one," but as it turns out, it translates to something like "Ah dammit."

Monica stepped out of the restaurant, following the commotion. "Michael?" she called. Her white blouse moved behind the vines hanging around the awning. "Are you drunk?"

"I'm fine."

"*Esta borracho*," Carmen clucked.

Monica came out from behind the vines, wiping her hands on a towel. She was a busty woman, all woman, and she didn't look happy. "You knew that you had to work tonight. Why would you do this?"

"We only had a couple." He shrugged and raised his palms like a martyr. "I'm fine."

"And you!" She looked at me. "You knew he was going to work tonight."

"He was buying. What was I going to do?"

"Tell him that he has to go to work."

"He told me that it was an emergency."

"It's always an emergency." She rolled her eyes and dropped her shoulders.

Michael started cursing in Spanish. I couldn't follow much of it, but I'm pretty sure he shouldn't have said it in front of his mother. Carmen's eyes got big. Monica folded her arms across her chest and pursed her lips. Michael gesticulated wildly. The tirade didn't end. Monica turned to walk back into the restaurant, Michael yelled louder. Then Carmen started yelling and Michael crossed his arms over his chest.

"Well, I think I might stagger home," I said.

Monica stopped and turned. "Oh, you're not going anywhere," she said. "If he's not working, you're taking his spot."

I looked at Michael. He fished his keys out of his pocket and opened the driver side door.

"Ah fuck you," I said.

He slid his sunglasses down over his eyes and got back in the driver's seat. Carmen banged her palm on the hood of the car and cursed at him. He shrugged at me and started the car.

"You bastard." I glared.

He flipped me off.

Carmen kept right on cursing in Spanish. It became gibberish to me, a staccato string of obscenities, most of which, I'm sure, she shouldn't be calling her own son.

Michael yanked the stick into reverse and jerked out of the parking spot. He punched it into drive and peeled out down the alley.

Carmen raged. She spun on me. "*Ay carajo borracho drogado*."

"*Watchale*," I said.

"Why you get him drunk?!"

"He called me," I said. "This is my day off."

"Now you work."

"It's my day off," I said, like maybe she missed that part.

"You got him drunk," Monica said, "So you're working." She still had her arms folded across her chest.

"He paid," I pleaded, but there was no arguing with either of these women.

"*Ya se fue, y tu tienes que trabajar*," Carmen said, and she didn't need to say much more.

I followed Monica in and pulled an apron from the rack. "Alright, let's do this thing." I fumbled with tying it around my waist.

Monica yanked a ticket from the window and set it into the rack. I finished tying on my apron as she called out appetizers, and, under the watchful eyes of two wrathful goddesses, pulled yucca from the fridge and started my prep. There was no room to fuck up, and yet, I got the feeling like I couldn't fail the test. If I was going to get fired, they would have to wait until my shift ended at least. Or rather, until Miguelito's shift ended. I dropped yucca into the fryer, pulled a clean plate to dress, and blinked sticky, drunken eyes at the prep line.

"Why would you get him drunk?" Monica asked, tossing a pat of butter into a frying pan. She was obviously undone.

"I didn't want to go, but he said that it was an emergency."

"It's always an emergency with him."

"Yeah, well I don't get much of a choice."

"What was it this time?"

I tried to busy myself with the plate, tried to ignore it.

"What was he whining about?" She tossed chopped garlic and shallots into the hot pan. They crackled and popped.

"Same stupid shit."

She threw in some sliced onions and a dash of salt, nodding as she flipped the contents of the pan.

"That stupid shitferfuck better get laid soon, or we're all fucked."

"Tell me about it." She tossed a fistful of steak into the pan and we both listened as it sizzled. She flipped the contents of her pan a few more times, deglazed it with some red wine, and stepped back as the flames died down.

Pop goes the Barbie

My roommate, Jenna, thought it might be good for me to get out and meet people again. She drove me down to the Saloon for a couple of drinks. I took a stool in the corner. Jenna bought a round. I bought a round. We smoked a few cigarettes. People came and went. The bar got packed. Somehow I got introduced to a little brunette. She knelt on the stool next to me and leaned in over the bar. She was in tight jeans and a pair of big bug-eyed sunglasses. "I want a drink," she told me.

"Good luck with that."

"Can you get me one?"

"Nope." I sipped my whiskey, sputtered, and took a sip of beer. "I'm broke," I said.

She leaned over the bar farther and watched the bartender. "I don't know this guy too well."

I raised my hand. Jeff came over. "This girl wants a drink. Could you get her one?"

He looked at me.

I shrugged.

"Yeah, sure," he said, and made her a vodka and tonic.

"So Jenna told me you got dumped." She stirred her drink.

"Yep."

"Me too." She took a sip and set the straw on the napkin.

"I guess that's why we're supposed to hang out."

She looked me over. "I guess you're cute enough. If you shaved and got rid of the sideburns."

"Thanks."

She leaned forward again. "Do you like my ass?" she asked and patted her butt.

I glanced over. It was nice. "Yeah, you have a nice ass."

"Of course you like my ass," she said. "Do you know how far I have to run each day to keep my ass looking like this?"

"How far?"

"Five miles." She took another sip of her drink and scooted closer. "You wanna touch my ass?"

Alright, so she's obviously hammered. "Sure," I said. I pulled a cigarette from my pocket. "You finish your drink. I'm gonna go smoke."

I squeezed through the crowd and out to the smoking section. Jenna was out there with a new boy toy. His name was Tom. He was a doctor of some sort. Nice guy, but a bit touchy-feely for me. He liked to put his hand on my shoulder or pat me on the back. If Habibi wasn't touching me, I didn't want anyone else touching me either. But I couldn't tell people this, or they would think I was really pathetic. Instead he put his hand on my shoulder and massaged it. "So what do you think of Melanie?" He grinned.

"She asked me if I wanted to touch her ass."

"What?!" Jenna laughed. "She must be drunk already."

Tom massaged my shoulder harder. "Well, go get her." He smiled.

I imagined the whole process laying itself out across the bare floor of the empty condo. I bring her home. There's nowhere to sit. I try to get her out of her clothes and fuck her drunk without falling out of the inflatable raft that works as a couch. Then I have to send her home, or cuddle. Buy her breakfast in the morning. Smile and kiss like it meant anything. Prove to my friends that I'm not desperately pathetic. It just didn't sound like my kind of evening.

"She just got dumped by her boyfriend," Jenna told me.

"Yeah, I know."

"I don't think she's looking for anything serious."

Really? Then why bother? I'm too broke for casual sex. "She's gotta be plowed," I said and glanced in. From the smoking section door I could see her kneeling on the stool, ass in the air. In the monkey kingdom, we call that presenting. It was indeed a nice ass. Can't imagine going jogging with her, though.

"We might head home," Jenna said.

"Yeah, fine. I'll find a ride somewhere." I finished my cigarette and walked back inside.

Melanie brushed shoulders with me. "You were gone so long," she said. "I was beginning to worry."

"Lung cancer takes a long time."

"Want to get out of here?" She smiled.

I think I had fantasies like this when I was fourteen. "Sure," I said.

"I'll be right back," she said.

She climbed carefully from her stool and made her way through the crowd. This is where she goes for her pimp or something. Maybe her ex-boyfriend was somewhere in the place.

Jeff slid down to my end of the bar. "That's Henry's ex," he said.

"Who's Henry?"

"He bartends down in the Lumberyard."

"Why'd he dump her?"

He raised his eyebrows. "She's crazy," he said.

"Me too." I shrugged.

"You want another one?" He pointed at my empty whiskey glass.

"Still broke." I shrugged.

"I got this." He poured a good glassful. "Watch out." He nodded at the girl making her way back through the crowd.

Melanie took her barstool slowly and gave me the fuck-me smile.

Jeff nodded his head, rapped his knuckles on the bar, and walked off. The guy behind me bumped me. I turned for a moment. Knew the guy from nights before. Said hello. Next thing I know the door guy's standing behind me. "You gotta get her out of here," he said to me.

Jeff was standing in front of me. "She's gotta go, Aaron."

I glanced over at Melanie. "Hon, they want us to leave." But I guess she already knew that.

She sputtered, lurched, and a trail of spittle ran from her lower lip. She didn't look so good anymore. Her gin and tonic had turned pink, and the bar in front of her was a puddle of pink puke.

"What the hell have you been drinking?" I asked. The door guy was helping her to her feet. "I barely know this girl," I said.

"Just make sure she gets home, wouldja?" Jeff asked.

I finished my drink. She took my arm and I steadied her out the door, holding her puke-stained purse. She stumbled on her high heels. When we got out the front door she puked on a newspaper box, steadied herself against the trashcan, and then puked at the feet of the people waiting in line to get into the bar. The pink was everywhere.

"Were you chugging Pepto Bismol, or what?" I said.

She clutched at my shirt, drooling pink. "Call my brother," she sputtered.

"I don't have a cell phone."

She collapsed on a public bench right in front of the Peruvian restaurant. She hunched forward and started puking on her high heels. The outside tables looked on, horrified. She lurched again and pink splattered across her shoes. I couldn't imagine where it was all coming from. On my best binge, I couldn't produce half that much puke.

Barry, the headwaiter, came out with a bottle of wine for one of his guests. I borrowed his cell phone. It took her a few lurches to get her brother's number out. A few minutes later he pulled up alongside the curb. By that point she was just dry heaving. We carried her to the car. "Thanks," he told me, and they drove off.

I wasn't always a loser. I mean, thinking back, there must have been a time when I showed some sort of promise. Somebody, years ago, must have told me that I was something special. It must have been young enough that it stuck, some childhood prophecy of predestination, the seed of greatness planted in the soil of a mind long since turned fallow. Maybe, decades ago, I was the apple of someone's eye, but staggering home from the Saloon a few minutes after last call, I was nobody, and nobody saw me.

It was just as well. Better to not be seen. Wobbling on rubbery legs, watching my pink puke splattered shoes, muttering to myself. I didn't mind so much. As a man stuck in a rut, it didn't seem like such a terrible place.

Sure, there were changes. Things happened. Somebody quit at work, and somebody else replaced them. Somebody moved away, somebody else moved in. Friends got married, settled down, had babies. Friends died and vanished from my life. I got kicked out of school. The girlfriend dumped me. Instead of going home to cook dinner and discuss the day, I staggered down a dark street toward an empty apartment, to rifle through the fridge for edible leftovers and fall asleep on a big yellow inflatable rubber raft in the living room, watching whatever was on TV.

There was no need to navigate, no need to steer, really. The rut provided everything, a sort of passive sense of direction, if ditches have any sort of direction. All I had to do was follow my feet, keep moving forward, the rut removed all doubt. Each day becomes pretty much the same as the one before it. Ruts provide a passive sense of security, a certainty, albeit terrifyingly boring, but certain nonetheless.

Seeing as how most people are so fond of security, I would think that ruts would be more popular. I'm sure that most people are stuck in ruts, although they don't know it. They call it a career, or a mortgage, or a life plan. They don't see it as a rut, they see it as safety.

All I had to do was follow my feet. Keep moving forward. The rut removed all doubt.

El Capitán, sin calzones

That guy had been out there since halfway through the dinner rush, at least. He had his radio turned all the way up, polishing the pep boys plastic chrome on his lowered Honda, blaring Mexican music, and trying to make out with his girl.

I was scrubbing down the line at the Peruvian restaurant, trying to get it cleaned up so that we could go home. Michael poured us a couple shots of pisco and wiped down the stove. Every few minutes he walked out back to talk to the guy. I don't know what they were talking about, but they'd laugh and slap each other on the back, and Michael walked back into the restaurant.

"So, *Guapo*, what do you say we go to Vegas?" he said. It was payday, so we both had checks in our pockets.

"I don't want to go to Vegas," I said.

"Ah come on. It'll be great." He smiled.

He poured us a couple more pisco shots.

"Why do you want to go to Vegas so bad?" I asked.

"Hookers, man."

"I'm not driving to Vegas to get a hooker."

"Javier needs to get up there for a wedding. He wants a ride."

Javier must be the little Mexican guy out back. "Fuck him. He's got a car. Let him drive his own ass to Vegas," I said.

"He's illegal."

"So?"

"So there's a border checkpoint. He'll get arrested."

"So you want to get arrested instead?"

"No. We'll just drive to the checkpoint, see if there's anyone there, and if there are guards, we'll just drive back here."

It sounded simple enough, but Michael had a way with the bait and switch. "Not tonight, Miguelito. I want to go home."

"Alright, fine." He walked out back and talked to Javier for a minute. They talked and laughed and the guy walked off. Michael came back in. "Want to go get a shot tonight?"

"Sure."

When I met him, Michael was top cock in the joint. Considering that it was run by his mom and sister, that wasn't saying much. He taught me to play fine-dining waiter, made me slow down, made me describe a dish like it was food porn. We didn't serve beef kabob. We served a succulent prime cut Kobe beef steak, aji panca marinated, carefully cut and skewered, slow grilled over an open flame, to order. We didn't serve chicken with rice, we served a hand-pulled chicken breast served in a savory garlic sauce over the old family recipe of garlic- and shallot-infused wild rice. The only real difference between shit on a shingle and gourmet cuisine is the time you put into describing it. Honestly, Michael and I worked the kitchen and the front on different days. Whether we were working the front of the house or the back of the house, we could have made shit on a shingle look and sound gourmet. Just the same, we didn't serve shit on a shingle.

Me, I was a cook. They gave me a recipe, I sliced, diced, julienned, and sautéed the hell out of it. But Michael, he understood the recipe. He knew the dish back to front, and understood what made it work. He grilled me harder than he grilled anybody, because those recipes were important. Too much garlic, too much shallot. The butter was burnt, or the grill marks were wrong. That guy knew what he was doing, and he rode me hard. Not because he cared so much. At least, he'd never admit it. He rode me because his mom and sister rode him, and so he had to ride me. That's where it got funny.

Whatever I fucked up, he caught hell for. The spinach was overcooked, or the medium went out medium rare. It was a few seconds over the fire, either way, and he got grilled for it. Working in a kitchen does funny things to a guy. Working with your mom and sister does something even funnier. At least, that is, it's funnier for the rest of us to watch.

Of course, I was a drunk before I started working there, and he wasn't exactly a bastion of sobriety, but when you spend enough time riding out the adrenaline rush of a busy kitchen, that shift beer looks better and better with every ticket passing through the line. After a three-thousand-dollar night, a shift beer goes better with a shot, and if we got yelled at about a plate coming out slow, or an appetizer that wasn't presented quite right, the shot and the beer could double or triple themselves pretty quickly.

I felt bad for the guy. I mean, it wasn't my restaurant, so I did the best I could, but it wasn't Michael's restaurant either, and the best he could do just wasn't good enough. He worked constantly, in the restaurant early to prep, and worked the line or the floor until close. Six days a week. He didn't have friends or a girlfriend, and he didn't exactly have a lot of time to find them, either. He had the Brazilian dishwasher and a liquor-stinking second cook for companions. Sure, I could go drinking, but I was falling out of love like a satellite falling out of orbit, burnt to a crisp and aiming for impact.

So this was Michael, beat down daily by his Mom and sister, working long hours over the stoves or pushing plates on tables begging to pay too much for Peruvian poverty food. I guess, when you see him this way, it's easier to understand why the guy was ready to risk jail time running illegals across a checkpoint, or a kidney to lose his virginity. He didn't really have a lot more going for him.

We finished up, locked the doors and after a quick stop at the liquor store to cash our checks, wandered over to the Saloon, followed by Joao, the dishwasher. He didn't drink, and he was Brazilian, so nobody understood what the hell he was saying, but he followed us anyway. Most of the time he just sat around with us, muttering in Portuguese and trying to convince Michael to roll a joint.

The Saloon was just starting to get busy, bodies filling stools and a few standing behind them. Michael waved at Jeff, the bartender and walked down the bar playing his sort of crapshoot playboy, duck-duck-goose game. As he walked by the girls sitting at the bar, he'd smile at them and hold a hand over their head. "One for her, one for her, one for her, *nothing* for her, she's got a boyfriend, one for her, and one for her." Jeff would line up shots of something girly, surfers on acid or redheaded sluts or whatever, and set one in front of whoever Michael had chosen. By the time we hit the far end of the bar, there were a couple of drinks waiting for us, and a line of Michael's hopefuls looking surprised and raising their shot glasses at us. As often as he did this, you'd think it might have gotten him somewhere by now, but he was still as chaste as ever, and a hundred dollars into the night, he was no closer to losing his virginity.

After six shots, Michael had called me every name he could think of, and I still wouldn't change my mind about going to

Vegas. But by the seventh shot I was breaking down, getting surly. I defended my honor with stories of my past pirate escapades. This was a mistake.

Michael leaned in with the final shot. "A real pirate would smuggle illegals," he told me. "You ain't no fuckin' pirate."

"The hell I'm not," I charged. "You know who I am? I'm Cap'n Noskivvies. I was captain of the great ship Stella Maris."

"Sure you were." He rolled his eyes.

"We stole eight cars in one night."

"When?"

"I fought a god once."

"And you're afraid to play *coyote*?"

A half-hour later, we were in front of his house, waiting for Javier and Pilar to show up. He lit a little pinner joint and we smoked it leaning back against the car.

"You realize this is a terrible idea," I said. We were both pretty hammered and smoking pot on top of that. If we made it all the way to the checkpoint without getting pulled over it would be a miracle. Assuming that we would make it all the way to Vegas was just stupid.

He shrugged and took a pull at the joint. "Beats sitting around here for another night."

La frontera

"Because they're not gonna pull over a little white kid in a red sports car. That's how," I said.

"That's loco. I get tickets all the time in this thing."

"Yeah, but driving through an immigration checkpoint, we don't fit the profile of *coyotes*. We're just another car on the way to Vegas." I hopped out and walked around the car. "Nobody would be stupid enough to smuggle illegals across a border checkpoint in a little red sports car."

Michael got out and pulled a blanket from the back. "And what are you going to do if they pull us over?"

"Jail time. Fuck, I don't know, man. They're not going to pull us over." I adjusted the seat and mirrors. "They're not looking for us."

"Can you even drive?"

"I had just as much to drink as you did." I pulled on my spectacles for effect. Clean and neat draws no heat.

Michael shook his head. "You really think we can do it?"

"I'm sure there's no way to drive this car through that checkpoint twice. It's too high profile and they're bound to get suspicious the second time around." I glanced back at Javier and Pilar. "And I don't think it's a good idea to leave the kids standing by the side of the road a few miles from an immigration checkpoint."

He turned to the backseat. "*El pinche gringo loco piensa que podemos pasar ahora. Que dices, si o no*?"

They murmured for a moment. Javier leaned forward and caught my eye in the rear view as he talked to Michael. "*Estan pendejos, pero vamos a intentarlo*."

They both sat back and buckled up. Javier nestled into Pilar's shoulder and pulled the blanket up to his chin. "*Vamonos pinche gringo*."

"They think you're fuckin' *gringo loco*, but they say go."

"What do you think?"

"I think the car gets impounded, we get a fat fine, they get deported, we do jail time. These guys are serious since 9/11."

"Your car, *Joto. Si o no?*"

"Go."

I started the car and flipped on the lights. "Rock 'n' roll."

"For the record," he said, pulling cigarettes from my shirt pocket, "I think you're nuts, too."

"Noted. I'm sure that the judge will be glad to hear that." I rolled through the gears up the onramp. "Find us a rock station. Pop rock, or something like that." He pushed buttons on the console. Yellow lights flashed on the signs warning slow speeds for the checkpoint two miles ahead. The passage itself was brightly lit with spots and fluorescents, carving a light gateway around the freeway. Brake lights stacked deep up to the light. The guards were stopping people. Vegas or jail time.

Michael cursed under his breath. "*Ay carajo gringo borracho pendejo. Tu estas loco.*"

"English, fucker." I tapped the brakes. A mile to go. "Think 'stupid fucking white guys.' Make it your mantra." There was no way to turn around. Blinking yellow lights on a yellow diamond crossing sign. A family of silhouettes frozen, fleeing across the roadway. Like deer signs, or cattle crossings, but a fuckin' family, dragging junior by his wrist they're running so fast.

"This is stupid, *Guapo*."

"A little positivity here, Miguelito."

We could see the agents.

"Better get down," he motioned to the backseat. Javier nestled deeper into Pilar.

"Let 'em sit up." I rolled down my window and hung an elbow out. Brake lights were slow. "We got *nothing* to hide. These kids are going to Vegas to get married."

"They're not getting married, they're just going for a wedding."

"Whatever."

The agents held traffic while a big brown van squeaked across a few lanes of freeway for secondary inspection.

"We are so fucked." He took a sharp drag off his cigarette.

"This is a hallowed mission, Miguelito."

"We're going to jail, *Guapo*."

"We're on our way to join these kids in holy matrimony. We're on a mission from God, man."

"They're not getting married, *Joto*. They're going for a fucking wedding and so he can get a fucking job. That's it. There is no mission from God."

"Yeah, well, when I tell it, they're gonna get married. And when I tell it, this is a damn holy mission. And when I tell it, we're gonna make it."

"*Estas loco, güero.*"

I bobbed my head to the music. "Repeat after me: These are not the droids you're looking for." And I waved my hand with a flourish.

"You're fuckin' nuts."

"Do you believe that rock 'n' roll can save your immortal soul?"

Traffic inched forward.

"What?"

"Yes or no, Miguelito."

We could see the agent's face. He was Mexican, or ex-Mexican. Brake lights stacked up like roller coaster cars ticking toward the drop.

"Sure." He shrugged.

"I couldn't hear you over the music, Miguelito. I said do you believe that…"

"Yes motherfucker, just drive."

The car ahead passed. "Well hallelujah, then." I rolled ahead, laughed nonchalantly, and glanced up at the agent, looking only mildly annoyed.

Fugitive Love

We sat at a Denny's a few miles north of the checkpoint. Javier and Pilar were hungry. My drunk was wearing thin, and Michael's, too. The trucker speed was kicking in. I can't believe they can sell that shit at gas stations.

"It's mind over matter, Miguelito. You just have to believe."

"Easy for you to say. I have a file folder of tickets."

"You want them." I shrugged.

"*Chingate guey*. I do not want tickets."

"You must, otherwise you'd quit speeding all the time."

"I don't look for tickets."

"I say you choose your life. Every fucking moment you decide. Do you want to be a victim of the California penal code, or can you decide to quit speeding and consider that lesson over?"

"Shit, *Guapo*, if it'll get me out of my tickets, I'll call the whole thing over."

"You say it, but you do not do it."

"Fuck you, motherfucker." He leaned forward. "Do you really think I want to spend the rest of my life paying off speeding tickets?"

"Then what do you want your life to be?"

"I want to be rich, motherfucker. I want a hot centerfold bitch on my arm and money in my pocket."

"You say that now, but get you drunk and stoned and you're talking about living on a farm in Peru, raising kids."

"It's a little more realistic, at least."

"Fuck realistic. What the hell is the point of freedom if you can't actively use it? People need to believe in something better. They need to believe in something big enough to get lost in, so they can forget the rest of it for a while. Love does that for people. Love is that powerful."

"But you're talking about something that's unattainable."

"No. I'm talking about real, visceral love. I'm talking about flesh and blood. Falling asleep beside her and waking up the same way, every damn day for the rest of your life because you like it better that way. There's no reason we can't have that sort of love. We're not supposed to, that's all."

"It doesn't exist, man. I'm twenty-five."

"All that means is that you haven't found it yet."

"We're going to Vegas, and I'm going to get a hooker."

"Fine, get a fucking hooker. I'll chip in. Maybe we can cut out this stupid self-destructive shit for a while."

He laughed. "And then what will you do with your free time?"

"Join AA, maybe take up macramé."

"Fuck is macramé?"

"The hippy art of knot tying."

"What?"

"I'm going to drive the motorcycle to Emira and get her back."

"Fuck does that have to do with knot tying?"

"I'm going to get her back."

He shook his head and laughed. "She ditched you, *Guapo*."

"That's fine. She's just too far away right now. She gets the fear and starts to do stupid shit, like break up with me. But when I'm close, she knows I'm close. She likes me close."

"She dumped you," he said, slowly, like I was missing something.

"So what?"

"So what happened to the 'this time it's over for real' bullshit you were flinging last week?"

"I don't want it to be over."

"She left you."

"You keep saying that like it's going to change something. Look, Miguelito, when you're in this kind of love, together or separate becomes negligible. You don't untie love like a shoelace. It takes a while. And this sort of love is gonna take a while longer."

"Prove it, *Guapo*. You go get the girl and then we'll talk about it." He patted his belly. "I think the coffee is kicking in. I'm going to take a shit." He set a twenty on the check.

Javier dug in his pocket for money and set it on the check. He said something to Pilar and followed Michael to the restroom. Pilar pulled the napkin from her lap and refolded it.

"I think it is very romantic," she said.

"You speak English?"

"I was born in Escondido."

"You haven't said a word this whole time. I thought you were illegal."

"No, just Javier." She pressed her napkin flat on the table, smoothing out the crumples. "But you can write it however you want. It sounds romantic. I just wish it were true."

"We're smuggling you and your boyfriend across a border checkpoint in the middle of the night. What's not true about that?"

She shrugged. "I'm not in love like that."

"But you'd like to be?"

She smiled. "Perhaps."

Javier came back to the table. He hung his arm around her neck and pulled her to him. It was more a headlock than a hug, but he kissed her cheek. "*Podemos ir a Las Vegas*?" he asked.

"*Si.*" I finished the last of my coffee, slapped a few bucks on the check, and we made our way to the front of the restaurant. Outside, I lit a cigarette and watched Javier try to kiss on Pilar. He had her backed up to the side of the car and whispered things under his breath. She giggled and feigned pushing him off

Vegas sucks ass

We woke up in a casino parking lot like the dead rising from the grave. The trucker speed left us wrecked, all rattling bones, hyper senses, paranoia, and things moving in the periphery. I had to pee so bad it hurt, and I wasn't sure I could make it all the way across the parking lot without pissing my pants. Michael kept muttering about the bunny ranch and a bloody Mary. We hadn't been in Vegas more than a couple of hours but already looked like shit, still in our work uniforms, stinking of Peruvian food, sweating pisco and tequila.

We made our way in through the back doors and pushed through the bodies to the first set of restrooms we could find. I stood at the urinal for what seemed like hours. Methamphetamines do the same thing. Gotta pee, but the stream is weak, and so I stood there with a dull throbbing pressure in my bladder.

Michael stood at the wall of sinks, giving himself a birdbath. He had his shirt off, hanging over a hand dryer. He splashed water up under his armpits, rubbing them down with hand soap, and working his way up to the mess of hair. "You got a bladder like a girl," he said.

"Fuck you, man." I pushed, but it wasn't doing much good. "I got yer ass out here."

"If I'd known you were going to waste the whole day at a urinal, I wouldn't have asked you."

"You wouldn't have found anybody else crazy enough to do that."

"True." He slicked his hair back and tied it into a curly shrub on the top of his head. "I still can't believe we made it."

"Mind over matter."

"You're a lucky fuck, that's all."

"That, too." I buttoned my fly and walked over to the mirrors. "Goddamn I look like shit."

He laughed. “Let’s get a few cocktails in you. You’ll feel better.”

I’ve never been a big fan of Las Vegas. I’m not a high roller, didn’t even have the money to fake it, and somehow wild sex in Sin City always made me wonder if I would wake up in a bathtub full of ice, missing a kidney, with a cell phone duct-taped to my hand. Maybe it was an urban legend, but if a night with a hooker was going to cost me a few days’ wages and a major organ, I’d just as soon skip it.

Michael though, he was a different story. In spite of the fact that I got the feeling he was bluffing, his constant talk of Vegas hookers had me wondering if he was really serious about going through with it. And whereas, in the past, we were generally too drunk to follow through with his plan, too drunk to make the drive all the way to Vegas, this time, we actually made it, and with some money in our pockets.

We took a seat at the back bar. Set into the bar itself were video slots, and behind the bar, a big screen TV played keno results. The bartender was a middle-aged man in a red vest, drying glasses with a bar towel and watching the numbers pop up on the screen like it was his favorite show. He set down his glass and walked over to us, setting a cocktail napkin at each of our spots. “What can I get for you gentlemen?”

Michael shrugged at me. “A couple bloody Marys.”

The bartender nodded and stepped off to pour.

“You look miserable, *Guapo*.”

“Feel like hell.”

“What’s the matter? You aren’t glad to be in Vegas?”

I glanced around at the empty bar. From the casino floor we could still hear the mechanical binging noise, see the blinking lights and the bodies milling between machines like the undead wandering lines of tombstones. “Not really.”

“Everybody likes Vegas.”

I shook my head.

“What the hell is wrong with Vegas?”

“What isn’t?”

The bartender set a little cocktail in front of each of us. They had the salted rim, the celery stick, the lime on the edge, a pimento-stuffed green olive, speared on a little sword. It was a booze infused salad in a little bucket glass. Michael grabbed his, raised it at me without much ceremony, and slugged half of it in a single pull. "This is the American dream," he said.

I looked at my cute little cocktail, poised a few inches from my lips, paused by his statement. "This?" I raised the glass at him.

He nodded and took another long pull, pretty much finishing off his cute, little cocktail.

"Look around, man. Lights, bells, whistles. Hot cocktail waitresses in miniskirts. Machines that pour out money when you push the button. Twenty-four hour, all-you–can-eat buffets. This is the American fuckin' dream, *Guapo*." He slid his cocktail to the edge of the bar, nodded at the bartender, and raised two fingers. The bartender nodded back.

I took a sip of my bloody Mary. "This isn't the American dream, Miguelito. This is what's wrong with America right now. This is America turning on itself, the sort of cannibalistic self-consumption that's killing us while we sleep."

Michael eyed my drink and looked at me. "Dude, drink that." He pushed my cocktail back into my face. "You're a lot more fun to be around when you're wasted."

"Fuck you."

"Yeah, fuck you too. Just finish it."

The bartender set two more in front of us.

"Last night, you were all Jedi mind trick bullshit, telling me that I had to fight for what I believe in, and now this?"

"I'm sober now."

"Yeah, and I can't stand it." He slurped down half of his cocktail and waved the bartender over. "Can you get my friend here a couple shots of bourbon?"

"I can only serve one drink at a time. He needs to finish that one."

Michael looked at me. "You heard the man."

I chugged down my drink in a few quick slurps and picked up the next one. The bartender watched. I took that one in a few quick slurps. It was mostly tomato juice anyway. Michael smiled. The bartender set off to set up a couple of bourbon shots.

"I don't want to die in a box," I said.

"Relax, you'll probably die in a hospital anyway."

"No boxes."

"Alright, fine, *Guapo*. No boxes." He fished the olive out of the bottom of his glass and bit it off the toothpick. "Finish that. We'll go win us some hooker money."

The bartender set the bourbon shots in front of us. Michael watched as I did mine and held his like he actually intended to drink it. "Hey man," he said to the bartender, "Where does a guy go to find a hooker around here?"

The bartender looked at him like we just lost our license to drink. "This isn't the place, man."

Michael nodded. "Fine, fine. How about two more."

The bartender set another couple of shots on the bar as another casino employee, a big guy with an earpiece walked up to the other end of the bar. The bartender walked over to him, and the two of them eyed us. Maybe it was the hooker line, or the fact that we just pounded four drinks apiece in less than twenty minutes.

"I don't think I'm feeling the love here." Michael said.

I shook my head.

"Find another place?"

I shrugged.

Michael waved over the bartender. "How about two more."

The bartender glanced down at the security guy. "I think it might be better if you both moved on to another bar," he said.

"Fine, how about two more shots, for the walk?"

The bartender glanced down at the other end of the bar. The security guy nodded. The bartender poured a couple more and set them in front of us, along with a bill.

Michael picked up the tab and shook his head at me. "Fuck this joint," he said.

"How much?"

"Fuck it very much," he said. "So much for the American dream, huh?" He dropped sixty bucks on the bar, downed his shot, and patted me on the back. "*Vamonos, gringo*."

The Vegas sun was a little intense, even through sunglasses. Michael eyed the cards spread on the sidewalk. Like baseball cards but with some centerfold chick spread half-naked, a stripper name, and a couple of phone numbers on the back. He bent over to pick one up, looked her over, and dropped it again. A few steps farther, he picked up another. He shook his head and tossed the card aside. "What's with all the blondes?"

"You're not really going to call one of those girls, are you?"

"Come on, gringo, you want an adventure, or what?"

"Let's find another bar."

"Alright. You pay this time."

We walked into another casino and wandered through looking for the bar.

The problem was that this sort of half-drunk excursion passed for adventure. Instead of getting out of the box, we just jumped from one box straight into another. The hours between boxes were something, at least. Hitting the accelerator on an open stretch of desert highway was an impression of movement, a seeming escape. But instead of catapulting ourselves out into the unknown, we end up in one sterile, climate-controlled holding pen after another.

Michael walked ahead, checking out the blackjack tables. All I wanted was another bar. At the far end of the casino, he waved me over. We took stools at the bar and waited for the bartender to come over. He looked about the same as the last guy, but in a blue satin vest and with a mustache. Michael ordered a couple shots of tequila and turned around to face the casino floor.

"Whaddya say, *Guapo*? We win ourselves some money, get us a free room, and call in a couple of those girls."

"You do whatever you want, man."

The bartender came back around to see if he could get us a couple more. Michael leaned in. "Say, man, is it safe to call those girls on the little hooker cards out there, or is there a better place to go to find a hooker?"

The bartender glanced back and forth. "Don't call them hookers," he said.

"Fine, what do you call them?"

"They're call girls. Some of them are dancers."

"Alright, is it safe to call them?"

The bartender shrugged. "Don't know. I've never tried." He eyed our empty glasses. "Another round?"

Michael nodded.

The bartender poured a couple more and set them in front of us. We downed those, too. "Well, we're going to need a room," Michael said.

"Don't look at me, man. I think our bar tab is going to break me before too long."

"You drink too much."

"*Nothing* else to do here."

"Gamble. Win money. Get hookers."

"Fine."

I paid the bartender. I don't know what we were drinking, but it cost me almost forty bucks. At this rate, we should be on the way home in the next couple of hours, at least. I followed Michael out onto the gambling floor, and while he eyed the blackjack tables again, I searched for a row of nickel slots.

Walking through the middle of a Vegas casino, it's hard to imagine that there ever was a frontier; a time when this particular stretch of desert was a pioneer's personal hell, an ugly expanse of dry death march between the civilized east and the Wild West. There was a time when Americans weren't the pasty wads of flesh, sitting around, plugging money into machines, but rather the rugged individuals carrying rifles and carving a life out of the land. In the movies, on TV, they always show Vegas as some rich expanse of beautiful people winning, winning, winning. The men are all these classy bastards in suits, and all the women are long legs and short skirts. Vegas is a desert dreamland where we come to pull a lever and step up a few income tax brackets.

They never show the real Vegas, the poor bastards sitting around, vacant eyes and hollow stares. They don't show the pasty zombie faces parked at a machine, watching their savings drop a few credits at a time, or buying their way into an all-you-can-eat buffet so they can eat for three hours straight and stuff napkin-wrapped lobster tails into their purse.

Here, in the real Vegas, it's all blue hairs blowing their pensions so they can go home to eat cat food for a few more weeks. It's guys whose fat asses barely fit on the stool, punching big, blinking buttons with stumpy fingers and watching you out of the corner of their eye, like you might be fucking their luck with your presence. It's a husband and wife sitting side by side, without a word, for hours at a time. It's superstition, suspicion, and the implied never-ending prayer for that one perfect lever pull, button push, or straight flush. Please God, make me a winner, forever and ever, amen. And we push the button, and the wheels spin, and bells and whistles, that don't mean a thing. Disguise the fact that our credits just dropped a dollar and we are still losers.

I found a spot near the bar where the cocktail waitresses bustled by on a regular basis. Maybe I wouldn't win, but at least the waitresses might keep me in free cocktails. Free, that is, as long as I didn't count the money I was flushing down the machine one spin at a time.

It wasn't more than an hour before Michael walked up behind me, cocktail nearly drained, pink ice in the bottom of a chimney glass and a long, red cocktail straw sticking out the top. "Well, that's it," he said.

"You finally find a whorehouse nearby?"

The little blue hair sitting next to me looked over, alarmed.

"Nah." He slurped the last of the pink from the bottom of his glass. "I ran out of money."

"That didn't take long."

"Thought the dollar slots might pay off better."

"So much for getting laid this time."

The blue hair leaned away a little bit.

"Fuck it," he said. "Buy me a drink."

"Yeah, fine." I pulled a ten from the crumpled wad of bills in my pocket and handed it to him.

"How much you got left?"

"I dunno." I handed him the rest of the wad.

He stood behind me, counting out bills.

"Shit," he said, and handed me the bills, straightened and faced as if for the restaurant cash drawer.

"What?"

"Twelve dollars," he said.

"There goes that paycheck."

"We got a problem."

"Besides your virginity?"

"We don't have enough money to get home."

"Fuck."

The blue hair sitting next to me hit the cash-out button, pulled her players card from the slot, and glared at us as she got up from her stool.

"Well, now what the fuck do we do?"

"You gotta win, *Guapo*."

I watched the credits dwindle on my machine, no closer to a payout than when we stepped in the door. "Yeah, that ain't happening." I pressed bet max through the last couple of dollars in the machine, and we sat staring at the insert coin message flashing on the screen. "Okay, now we're fucked."

Michael found a pay phone near one of the exits. He leaned up against the wall, punching numbers into the phone. I couldn't hear him over the bells and whistles, but it was clear that Monica wasn't thrilled with the phone call. He yelled into the phone, and I'm assuming she yelled back. People walking by glanced over at him and only spoke to each other after they had passed him. Some snickered. Some looked nervous.

He strolled over from the pay phone angry. "Gimme a cigarette."

I handed him one. "What did she say?"

"She's going to transfer some gas money to my account."

"Are we in trouble?"

"What's this 'we' shit?"

Michael didn't look so happy anymore. Not really disappointed, but more beat down. If he'd really wanted to find a hooker, he hadn't tried very hard for it. Maybe he really was hoping to win a few bucks, but following him back down the Strip, he just walked along like he was pulled by a string. Whatever his sister had said to him, it was enough to take the fight out of him. We climbed back into the car and, without so much as a souvenir, made our way back to the freeway.

We were only a couple of miles out of Vegas when the rain started, light at first, just a drizzle on the windshield, until it started collecting. Michael hit the windshield wipers and the rain started dripping in through the open windows and rolling in through the open top.

Without the T-top glass, the sprinkle wasn't getting us too bad, but we both hunched over and hoped it would stop. It didn't. The rain got harder. Michael hunched farther over the wheel and I cupped my hand around my cigarette to keep it dry.

"Well, *Guapo*, you wanted an adventure," he said.

I glared at him.

As the rain got harder, he tried to speed up. We hydroplaned a little, so then he had to slow down. And we started getting really wet. "I think we're going to have to pull over," he said.

"And then what?"

"I keep a tarp in the trunk. We can cover up at least."

"Fine," I said.

We spotted a set of lights up ahead, another casino. He pulled into the far corner of the parking lot, jumped out of the car and pulled a dome tent rainfly from the trunk. We stretched it over the top, hooked it under the wheel wells and crawled in under it.

The wind came harder with the rain. Michael pulled a couple of the blankets out of the back and gave me one. We were already wet, but the blankets were pastel wool, from Tijuana. They made it easier, at least. I tucked in under mine, rolled myself in it, hoping that it might pull some of the damp out, but still I couldn't sleep too well. The front seat of a little red sports car, even with the seat laid back, wasn't much of a bed. I laid there for a while, listening to the wind whip up the rainfly, and the rain beat it back down. "So much for the American dream," Michael said. "We didn't even hit the buffet."

In spite of the blanket, I was shivering.

"Hey *Guapo*," Michael said, "would you consider this a box?"

I nestled into my blanket further, tried to ignore him. The wind ripped at the rainfly, and the rain beat it back down. It reminded me of camping when I was a kid, somewhere far away from civilization, far enough that I wondered if we would ever make it back. "No, Miguelito. No, this is definitely not a box."

"Okay, *Guapo*." He nestled deeper into his own wool blanket. "Goodnight, *Guapo*."

"Goodnight, Miguelito." I rolled deeper into my blanket, but it was a while before I could sleep.

Special-needs my ass

My parents' garage was as decent a shop as I could hope for, a complete tool set, a crappy stereo that played CDs sometimes, and the back fridge had beer in it. Repairing Rosinante gave me something to do, a way to keep my hands busy, and my head occupied with the Zen mystery of motorcycle mechanics. Since I never bought a manual and never really learned much about mechanics, repairs were generally a matter of figuring it out on my own.

I had the old turn signals off, rewiring the new ones, a couple of hot little low-profile pieces, drilling holes through the fairing, running in the grounds, and trying to reroute the wiring harness. The garage door was open, the radio on, and a bottle of pale ale was doing the trick. At the very least it kept me out of the condo, and far away from the Magic Marker writing that was bleeding down the mirrors, a little more with every shower.

The eldest girl from next door pushed a stroller up the driveway toward me. "Hi, Aaron. Whatcha doin?" She asked a lot of questions. It's the only way she knew how to engage people. She was almost sixteen but still had the mind of a ten-year-old. I'm not exactly sure why; she was just a little slow. As I hunkered down to inspect the wiring on the turn signals, she bent over to tie an old set of sneakers onto her ratty old teddy bear's feet.

"I'm fixing the lights," I said.

"Where's Emira?" she asked.

And whatever motorcycle Zen I had achieved two beers deep passed away in two words. "She's in Eastern Washington," I said.

"Well, why?"

Good question. Point goes to the special-needs kid. "She's visiting her mom."

"Well, why?"

Because I'm an asshole. "Because she misses her," I said.

"Well, when is she coming back?"

I didn't know how to tell her that she's not. "Don't know."

"Well, why not?"

They tell me that Zen is like a state of drunk, or like the mind of a child. It is openness, and apparently, that state of openness could be summed up in the word why. "She might stay there for a while."

"Well, when will she be back?"

She won't. "I have to go get her."

"Well, why don't you go get her?"

There's that why again. "I have to fix my bike first."

"Is this your murdercycle?"

"Motorcycle, Steph."

"I said murdercycle."

"Yes, this is my motorcycle."

"Well, what's wrong with it?"

"It's sick." Lovesick, really.

"Oh."

"I'm making it better."

"Oh." She petted her bear's head. "And then are you going to get Emira?"

"Yes."

"When will she be back?"

"Soon."

"Oh good." She petted her bear's head again. "Well, what's wrong with your murdercycle?"

It's got a broken heart. "Motorcycle, Steph."

"I said that."

I've played this game before. The point is to keep asking questions, first to make a statement loses a point. Thus far, I was getting my ass kicked by a special-needs kid with a teddy bear in a stroller. "Is this your baby?" I asked.

She looked down at the bear. He was dressed in her kid sister's old clothes and those big sneakers. He looked a little worn. "Yeah," she said.

Point goes to the beer-buzzed jerk with the screwdriver. "What's his name?"

"Kevin."

Another point. "He's cute."

"Yeah."

No point. "Is that your mom calling for you?"

"No."

Is that a point? "I thought I heard her calling for you."

"No."

"Well maybe you should go check."

"Mom is taking Kelsey to soccer."

"Alright, well, I'll see you later."

She looked a little confused for a second and then turned her stroller around. "Bye, Aaron."

"Yeah, Steph, bye."

She pushed her baby down the driveway.

I don't know which was worse, the other kids taking bets on the bike, or Stephanie calling it a murdercycle. It wasn't really helping. I stared at the dangling turn signal, the beer with the last few backwash gulps in it. The radio was playing some sad, sorry breakup song, some lovelorn, make-me-cry sort of piece. I stepped away from the machine, took a seat, and emptied the bottle. She had a point. Match goes to the special-needs kid with the bear in second-hand clothes.

Why? Why indeed.

The strange air at night

Mat stood squarely on both feet, cocktail held nearly to his chin, swirling the skinny cocktail straw around in his rum and Coke. He was in his work boots, black jeans, and a long-sleeve black shirt with hotrod flames running the length of his arms. He had his glasses on, thick black plastic frames like goggles. He glanced about, watching bodies fill in the spaces. He raised an eyebrow at a blonde walking by, but his expression was of a man taking in an old movie he's seen a hundred times. "There's something strange in the air tonight," he said.

I followed his gaze, but I couldn't pick it out. "Like what?"

He shrugged. "I don't know." He checked the pool tables. "There's just something strange."

I was a little past stoned and already buzzed, so watching the bar fill on a Friday night left me with the clinging outsider sensation anyway. I knew I didn't belong, but I needed the moving bodies. I don't much like the Saloon at night. Used to be that the place was packed when all the barstools were taken. Over the years, it became a popular dive bar in some local magazine poll, and then everybody wanted to slum it with the locals.

As the afternoon stretched into evening, the last of the old-guy regulars filtered out. And as evening writhed its way into night, the bar filled with younger faces. Twenties on up, but most of them college kids in brand-new blouses or club shirts, miniskirts or casual pants, corners smoothed, legs and faces shaved and lotioned, and the whole bar started smelling like a tincture of spilled beers, sweat under fresh cologne, and hair product. Hip, young suburbanites out for an evening, following their fight-or-fuck philosophies. It all starts to look the same after a while, a blur of bodies and faces.

Halfway to the bottom of my second cocktail, it occurred to me that, indeed, something wasn't right, like one of the stained-glass lamps behind the bar was off or the jukebox was only playing out of the left speaker or something. There was definitely something strange in the air that night.

Mat was the sort of guy that should be getting more ass than he actually was. He had all the right toys, the chopper out front, the chopped classic Caddy in his driveway, the tattoo gig, and he practiced art like it was some sort of geek fu. He had the look down pat, red hair slicked back under his black beanie and black plastic glasses, his arms discreetly hidden under long black sleeves. He didn't know anybody either, but he wouldn't sit at the bar, so he stood behind me. He was as good as a shadow, chuckling and muttering wisecracks under his breath.

"Hey, check it out." Mat pointed down the bar at a spent-looking waif of a bleach blonde. "Paris Hilton's here." It was a game he liked to play, picking celebrities out of the living dead.

"I'm going to go down and ask for her autograph," I said.

"You should."

"Yeah, right after this drink." I pulled my pint glass closer.

"What do you think these people do?"

"I don't know, crawl back into their parents' graves during the daylight hours."

"Do they work?" Work to Mat was something completely different. His jeans and boots were still covered in aluminum dust from working in the chopper shop all day. He made things, with his hands, and people gave him money for it. The concept of a credit swap generation made no sense to him.

"They consume. That's their job. Eat, shit, sleep, fuck, buy, and spend the rest of their waking life watching television."

He grumbled. "I should have a trust fund."

"I'm too young to die."

"You could drink all day long."

"I already do."

He eyed the mirror. "Check this guy out."

A body materialized out of the mass, squeezing past Mat to slide up next to me at the bar. Mat's reflection shook his head at me from the mirror behind the bar.

The guy was some striped shirt type, hair coifed up, reeking of some body spray. He wore white framed sunglasses in a dark bar, with a neatly trimmed little first time mustache that made him look perfect ready for a vodka add. He stood there for a few seconds, nodding his head. "Hey," he said.

"Hey," I said.

He had his credit card out and tapped it against the bar in front of him. Jeff walked past him twice. Mat smiled from over the guy's shoulder.

On the third pass, Jeff looked at the guy and then at Mat and me. The guy pushed his credit card at Jeff. "Can I get four shots of tequila, a vodka tonic, and two redbull and vodkas?"

Mat shook his head and turned away.

Jeff nodded, took the guy's credit card, and turned back to the well.

We watched Jeff run through his pours, stack up glasses at the edge of the rail, and ring the kid up for just over fifty bucks in cocktails. After the kid signed his slip and took his first round of drinks out to the table, Jeff showed us the slip. The guy tipped five dollars on all those drinks. The kid came back, grabbed the rest of the cocktails, and nodded at us both.

Mat watched him duck into the crowd with the last of the drinks in his hands, pushing his way back to his cluster.

"He must model for Old Navy," Mat said.

I just shook my head.

"How much do you think he pays to get his hair done?"

"More than I got to spend on parts."

"Why don't you just quit coming in here, save your money, and buy a decent fucking Ducati?"

"I should be on the road already."

He rolled his eyes. "That thing's a piece of shit."

"But it's mine."

"Why don't you just save some fuckin' money and buy a decent fuckin' bike?"

This was his constant complaint. I couldn't tell if it was a sales pitch, or optimism.

"Can't afford it."

He looked at my drink and then at me. "Want to play some pool?"

"Nah."

He swizzled the straw around his glass. "I'm going to play some pool." He turned and slid into the crowd of fresh-pressed zombies. I watched him slide back toward the pool table. The living dead laughed and smiled and looked like they were having a good time. Maybe there was something wrong with me, maybe I was the living dead, but they just didn't seem real.

We shouldn't be here.

But the bike wasn't back together yet, and Habibi was still on radio silence.

She left you weeks ago.

She was just too far away.

At least if she came back, she'd know exactly where to find you.

I finished my cocktail and slid it to the rail. Jeff walked up and picked up the glass. "Can I get a half-caf Mcfrappuccino, Jeff?"

He nodded and refilled it with rum. "Weird night," he said.

"Yeah."

He looked down the bar. "Where is everybody?"

The place was packed, but none of them regulars.

"They're smart. They stayed home."

There was a commotion in the crowd, a pool stick rose out of the sea of bodies, a fin edging up on its prey.

"Shit," he said. The bouncers slid from the door, dark wads making their way back to the pool tables. Bodies pushed and seethed.

Mat slid up next to me again. He slurped down the rest of his cocktail. "I'm getting out of here," he said. "Some guy just tried to hit me with a pool stick."

"Really?"

He set his glass on the bar and nodded. "Later."

Somebody shoved me. When I turned around it was one of the guys that I'd been drinking with the day before. "Some guys are about to beat up a chick out front," he said, grinning.

"Fuckin' zombies." I got to my feet and pushed my way to the front smoking section.

The blonde had her back to the picket fence, purse held at the ready, and her left fist ready for a sloppy jab. A half-dozen guys surrounded her, penned her in. She screamed at one guy and he screamed back and stepped forward.

I leapt, stepping off the picket fence, and cleared the blonde's shoulder, landing between her and the guy. The bodies eased back, surprised, at the very least, by the entrance. I glanced back at the blonde. "Aaron!" She threw her arms around my neck and fell against my back, choking me out with her practiced Southern charm.

The guy in front of me laughed. "She's your problem now, man."

I wanted to take back the leap. I wanted to be at the bar with my drink, strictly uninterested in the strange air, or better yet, back at the condo with a bowl, a bottle of my own rum, and anything for mixer. I wanted to be anywhere else.

"My hero!" she said and clung even tighter.

"Wait," I implored the guy. "Hold on a second."

"No fuckin' way, man. That bitch is crazy."

"I'm crazy?! I'm crazy?! You used me!" She hissed and clawed over my shoulders at him. I found myself holding her back. I wanted to be anywhere else.

"She's your problem now." A couple of the other guys laughed.

"Fuck you, you pig! You filthy pig!"

"Just let him go, Darlene."

"Four years, and when I was in trouble, you flew out of the air like Superman!"

"Aw fuck."

"This man is a gentleman. He wouldn't fight with a lady!" she called over her shoulder. One of the guys at the front door laughed.

"Just put your shit together. I'll walk you home."

Darlene Temple was arguably one of the hottest girls I ever slept with. Long blonde hair, big firm tits, a round ass, and an all-over tan. She had California girl down to an art, despite the fact that she was from the South somewhere. She did beach bunny like it was *Gone with the Wind*, always screwing up her courage to be an independent woman and fainting out into the arms of whichever guy was nearest.

"What happened to you?" She pulled her purse up her shoulder and brushed the loose blonde hair out of her eyes with a flat palm. She seemed to get drunker by the minute.

"I, uh…" What in the hell had I been doing for the past four years?

"You vanished. I looked everywhere for you."

"Well…" I couldn't decide where to start, the night that I walked off the face of the planet barefoot? The fire troupe? The pirates? The endless space of unknowing that lay between us? No matter what I said, it would sound insane.

"I kept your shoes under my bed for four years, waiting for you to come home."

"Why would you do that?"

"It's a Voodoo secret."

"Did it work?"

"You flew out of the air like Superman to rescue me."

"I wish you'd quit saying that."

"It was so," she leaned into me, "valiant."

"Oh god."

She threw her arms around my neck and pulled me close. She reeked of beer and smoke. "I've missed you so much, Aaron."

"Oh for fuck sake, we only dated for a few weeks."

"But you came back." She kissed my ear, my cheek, working toward my lips. As I pulled away she grabbed my head, tried to hold me in place, but I had her off balance.

"Come on," I said. "Let's get you home."

"You came back."

I took her arm and led her up the street. "Do you still have my shoes?"

She shook her head. "I threw them away a few months ago." She looked like she was about to cry. "I'm sorry, Aaron. I didn't want to, but I had to move on."

"Damn. Those were good shoes."

Javier returns

Miguelito, Joao, and I snuck hits off a carrot pipe, blowing the smoke up the hood fan and drinking Cusqueña Negra. Joao kept going on in Portuguese about the weed in Brazil. He pushed his glasses up on his nose and went on about *une bombe*, describing some mythical joint and the friends he smoked it with. Michael followed enough Portuguese that he could keep up and kept chuckling back some stilted amalgam of Spanish. Joao looked me dead in the eye, wrapped his fingers around an impossible object, and nodded. *"Une bombe."* I guess I got enough of it. Once upon a time, in a faraway land, he smoked a joint as big as my arm.

Jesus worked around us, shaking his head at us. He didn't much like the *mota* and probably didn't like watching us slow down our close with every pass of the pipe. Michael was doing his best to keep Jesus in beer, and a forty-minute close worked its way into an hour or so, with all of us out back, leaning back in our chairs, cussing at each other in Spanish.

When the headlights flashed across the back wall of the restaurant, Michael sat up and set his beer down, just in case it was his sister. A car door swung open, spilling loud Mexican music out into the alley. Michael leaned back again. A minute later, Javier stumbled into the doorway. He practically fell into the case of beers, and the chairs moved around to make space. He wasn't making much sense to me, but it wasn't important. Michael kept nodding, laughed a few times, and once, we all raised our beers to him.

"What the fuck is he doing back here?" I asked.

"His girl is pregnant," Michael said. "I think he's looking for work."

"What the shit, man? We just dragged his ass out to Vegas so he could come back a few days later?"

"They're pregnant," Michael said again.

"Well at least somebody got laid in Vegas."

Michael laughed.

We finished off the case of beer celebrating with Javier. At some point, somebody ran over to the liquor store to get a bottle of tequila and another case of beer, and we managed to get most of the way through both of those. By the time we started moving toward the doors, we were all pretty well hammered.

We walked past the Saloon, late enough and enough shots in all of us that not one of us was thinking about going in there. The bodies flowing out were thick, and somebody brushed up against Jesus, harder than Jesus liked. He spun on his heels and threw his arms up in the air. "*Que chingados*?" The big guy turned around as well and then everything became a blur of bodies. The big guy went straight into Jesus, they both went over, and the rest of the bodies poured out of the Saloon or off the sidewalks, into a puddle of club shirts and work pants, arms and legs flailing, swinging at anything that moved.

I remember standing in the middle of it, trying to pull Jesus off the guy under him, only to get punched in the back of the head and go down over a heap. Then there were legs moving and bouncers pulling us apart, only to stumble ten feet down the sidewalk and into yet another haystack of Hollywood roundhouse punches. *Nothing* made its mark, and I think the guys on the bottom were so busy tripping over each other that they had lost a mark entirely. Again the bodies shifted, and fumbling down to the front of 7-Eleven, the random swinging mass kept up their kinetic dance. Faces came out of the fray with this strangely similar look of surprise, arms gripping or swinging away, but always amazed, panicked, confused.

The sirens came at the street corner, and the mass exploded in people running away. Across the intersection, down the alley, back toward the Saloon. Maybe they were just random drunks, but the minute the cops appeared on the scene, the bodies scattered.

I was off down the street and slid behind a storefront into the hedges lining the sidewalk. I hit another body on the dive, he caught me and propped me back up, holding me flush against the wall.

"What the fuck?" I whispered.

He held his fingers to his lips and leaned back. The sirens swam past, red-and-blue lights casting Christmas branch shadows against the wall behind us.

I recognized the guy next to me from nights before, thought I was doing shots with him a few days earlier, but I didn't know him well. He shook his head. He had blood around his nose and smeared it across his cheek with the back of his hand.

"You're bleeding, man." I pointed at his wrist.

"Fuck," he said. He wiped his wrist on the leg of his slacks and leaned forward to wipe his nose on his knee.

"Fuck, man, what the hell was that?" I wiped my nose, to see if there was any blood, but there wasn't.

He shrugged. "I don't know." He wiped his nose again and checked it. "I didn't even know that guy."

"Then what the hell was that?"

He looked at me, maybe for the first time. "Say man, aren't you…"

"Yeah, man."

"What the fuck?" he said.

"That big guy hit Jesus, I don't know what the hell happened."

He glanced out from under the bushes, crouching down low. "I don't know, man."

"Clear?"

He nodded. "How's my face?"

Hiding behind the hedges, in the shadows, it was hard to tell, but the blood was mostly gone and any bruising hadn't started yet. "Fine," I said. "See you tomorrow?"

He nodded again, pushed through the bush, and stepped out onto the sidewalk, walking away from the police lights like a man minding his own business.

I wiped my nose, but I didn't find anything, no tender, tingling spots to indicate a blossoming bruise. Pushing out of the hedge, I started to follow the other guy down the street, away from the swimming red-and-blue lights, but seeing four or five officers standing at the corner, I figured somebody must have been caught.

I turned down through the alley, cut through a parking lot, and came up around the corner beside the Mexican restaurant. Walking down toward the police cars, I found four guys sitting on the curb in front of the officers.

Michael had his hands cuffed behind him, Joao had his head in his hands, Javier was slumped forward, and Jesus held a napkin up to his face. Two of the officers asked questions, another questioned a witness standing nearby, and the other two talked to people walking past.

"They attacked us!" Michael said to the officer.

The officer spoke into his radio.

"Sure, go ahead, blame the fuckin' Mexicans." Michael leaned forward and shook his head.

I was a few steps from Michael when an officer stopped me.

"You need to keep moving," he said.

"That's my boss," I said.

"Keep moving," the cop said.

"Look, I just need to talk to him."

Michael saw me. "Aaron! Tell them we didn't start it!"

"Keep moving," the officer said.

"They didn't start it. It was the guys coming out of the bar," I said.

The officer in front of Michael said something I didn't understand.

"Fine, so fucking arrest me, Pig! You got us on the curb because we're brown!"

"Look, can I just talk to him for a few seconds?" I asked.

Joao looked up at me, shaking his head. Jesus scowled. Maybe not at me, but he wasn't happy, and his face was already changing color, a big red spot under his eye turning purple. The napkin he held was dark with blood. Apparently he got hit pretty hard.

The officer leaned forward, "Unless you want to be sitting there with them, you got to keep moving."

Michael glared at the cop. The cop said something to him, and Michael turned to me. As the officer in front of me gently pushed my shoulder, Michael smiled, something dark and mischievous. "Call Monica," he said calmly. "Tell her I'm going to jail." He smiled wider, a look like satisfaction. The officer in front of him said something to him. Michael turned his grin on the cop. "So fuckin' Mace me you racist pigwhore." Joao shook his head at me again. I wasn't sure if he was even legal, or Jesus for that matter. Javier was illegal for sure, and there was a good chance that his girlfriend might be having the baby alone in Escondido.

The street fight might mean deportation for all of them, but there was *nothing* that I could do. The officer nudged me on again. I turned, following the push, and walked back down the street, away from the scene. Halfway down the block, I could still hear Michael yelling. "You racist pigfuckers had a dozen white guys you could be arresting, but instead, you gotta pick on the fucking Mexicans!"

I wasn't exactly sure how I was going to approach Monica with this, but I was fairly sure I was going to wake her up to do it. I walked a few blocks down and turned on third, making my way toward Monica's house. At the very least, I figured, I should do it in person. As I walked, I tried to replay the fight in my mind, tried to figure out exactly how I walked in and out without a mark, but none of it made sense. Through the adrenaline filter, it was all the bodies swinging, kicking, writhing, the shocked masks of faces caught up in the fray. Maybe nobody knew how or why. I didn't remember throwing a single punch, but up until that point, I had considered myself a bit of a badass, not the pansy-ass peacekeeper that walked straight through my first decent streetfight, entirely untouched.

Ascent

I drove back and forth between the Escondido cycle salvage and the San Marcos bike junkyard for a few hours, hunting for various bolts and brackets. Accidentally pocketed a chain adjust bolt from the cycle salvage while the guy was busy hunting down new pipes. He didn't have the stock pipes, but he had a two-into-one Yoshi exhaust for a hundred and twenty five bucks. It had a couple scratches from racing but I figured if I replaced those old rusted out pipes, Rosinante would get up and dance like a high school kid on ecstasy. Even if it might get me home that much faster, there was no way I could justify blowing a hundred twenty five dollars on a racing exhaust system.

The lady in the San Marcos shop took my busted footpeg bracket and disappeared for twenty minutes. I knew she was out back searching, but if she had just let me walk the yard, I would know if they had a wreck like mine back there in under five minutes. Used to be that her dad worked the front when he wasn't out back fixing something. The man knew his bikes. He looked like he'd been spun since the eighties; gnarled, leathery, with a pot belly and bad teeth. Must've been in that shop half his life, judging by the thick grease shellac on everything. He could have told me if they had that bike or anything close out back, but I hadn't seen him in years. His daughter ran the front now. She brought me a Honda bracket for the wrong side. "This might work." An inch of ash hung from the end of her Benson and Hedges menthol. I took my piece back and thanked her politely. Wished I could find her dad. Worn out chode smoker maybe, but at least he knew his parts. Guy actually had an old Indian in a shed out back, picture pretty, chrome everywhere. He was restoring it slow. Didn't get enough time to work on it, but I guess that was the direction his rut was taking him.

Made a few phone calls, and finally caught Mat in the shop, so I drove all the way out to Oceanside to grab the tank, down to Encinitas for forty-five minutes of traffic on the I-5. He cut the fairing tabs off the tank and even spot welded the foot peg bracket back together. He must've bitched for twenty minutes about the crappy low grade cast aluminum that Kawasaki used. He individually machined plenty of parts out of aircraft grade aluminum, and he was convinced that Kawasaki used ninety percent plaster of Paris.

I hated that bastard. He was building these sporty little Ducati choppers, had shelves lined with brand new chrome pieces, a shop space and all of the tools, and there I was trying to get a shitty Kawasaki piece welded so I could take my scrapper out for a ride. I hated him even more because he spent about an hour working on my ratbike and he didn't charge me shit. "Eh, buy me a drink." He said. But we both knew I probably wouldn't see him down at the Saloon again anytime soon. As decent as his weld looked, he told me that the metal was shit, and if it cracked once, it would probably crack again.

Made it back to my parents' garage just after dark. Found myself a bottle of beer, turned up the radio, and set back to making love to a motorcycle with a socket wrench, all the while fantasizing about Habibi. After a couple of hours work, there were a couple extra bolts, some sundry plastic pieces I cut off, and all those parts I replaced laying in a pile around her, but she'd ride if I rolled her down the drive.

Alone in the garage, Rosinante cast in the halogen glare, I watched my shadow pace beside me. *You'll never make it all the way to Eastern Washington.*

I climbed on, bent over the tank, twisted the throttle, and tried to imagine just what she'd sound like with the new pipe. When I shut my eyes I could feel the wind, the clinging to her back ecstatic. I could feel the girl getting closer.

She left you.

"I'm coming home, Habibi." Trying to hold that brief flicker of hope.

But as I was getting off the bike, the bracket cracked again.

Fuck it. It would hold for thirteen-hundred miles at least. After that, Rosinante was as good as a paperweight.

Armageddon babysitter

When Megan moved out of Joao's place, Michael knew it first, before Megan or Joao showed up to work. Of course, because I was standing next to Michael chopping onions when he got the call, I knew it, too. Jesus, if he understood any of it, didn't seem to care.

His face, a few days healed, still looked like he'd done a face plant into a brick wall, both eyes swollen, the bruises yellowing out at the edges. He'd had a few days off after the fight and came back into work with a chip on his shoulder. He worked surly, slamming pans around as he prepped, his puckered face stuck on permanent glare. For whatever reason, he wasn't happy with me, and the only reason he put up with Michael was because Michael actually got arrested that night, and the cops had eventually let Javier, Jesus, and Joao walk away.

Michael didn't have to do the three days in jail, but somehow, he managed to get himself pepper sprayed twice while he was in there, and the police said they wouldn't release him until he calmed down.

By the time his mother got to the courthouse to bail him out, he had given up on his racism tirade and realized that the only way out of the drunk tank would be to mind his manners. Even though I got the feeling like the few nights of calling the cops pigs had been exactly what he needed to fulfill his raging self-destructive streak, he wasn't terribly happy about the whole thing.

Up until he got the call from Megan, I figured I was going to get an ongoing lecture on the racist police state. But when he hung up, everything changed. He set up shots of pisco and passion fruit juice before we had the line set, long before either Joao or Megan walked in the front door.

Joao wasn't much of a drinker. He had some issue with his mother years before. From what I heard, he hit his mom one night while he was drunk, and he'd given up drinking ever since then. Nevertheless, he walked through the kitchen door ready to self-destruct. Seeing Michael standing there with a pisco bottle in one hand and that stupid half-Peruvian, shit-eating grin, he didn't much care what Michael was drinking to, so long as Michael was pouring for everyone.

"*Salu, dinero y amor*," Michael said, "and someone to enjoy them with." He smiled at me. Joao didn't respond. I didn't know whether he understood or not, but I assumed he must speak at least a little bit of English after living with a white girl for a few months. We raised our little steel ramekins of pisco and tilted them back. Joao finished his shot, flinched, and slapped the ramekin back on the counter. "*De novo*," he said, pushing his glasses up his nose. Michael shrugged at me and set up a couple more shots. For once in my life, I didn't much want the shot, but given the circumstances, there was no way out of playing third place in the kitchen pissing contest.

When Megan showed up to set up her tables, the kitchen got quiet. Joao washed dishes with his back to the line. I caught a couple of glances between Michael and Megan. If Joao caught any of the looks, he didn't say anything in English, but muttered to himself in Portuguese. But then, to me, it always seemed that he was muttering to himself in Portuguese, and I suppose I shouldn't have thought anything of it. A few times he turned around, banged his ramekin on the counter and demanded another shot. "*Un Novo*." We finished the bottle before the dinner rush started.

A fine-dining dinner rush is an adrenaline ride all its own. Assuming that *nothing* goes wrong, the whole damn kitchen is pretty much floating between red alert and all-out nuclear meltdown at any given point in time. Now, throw in one angry Brazilian with a broken heart and crank the fire to full. Toss in one Oaxacan with a busted face who is learning to hate white guys. Fling in a handful of white guy who walked out of a street fight involuntarily pretty and who is pretty well wasted. Deglaze with a one-half-Peruvian shitferfuck sancho who is secretly making time with the broken-hearted Brazilian's now ex-girlfriend. Toss in a lot of sharpened knives, some open flames, and a suddenly available white girl in the front, and one can only imagine the sort of tense, finger-on-the-button sort of adrenaline overload that we were all getting into. Now flip the pan a few times over the open flame, see who flips out. I'm still impressed that nobody got stabbed.

There were no jokes on the line that night, no subtle innuendos, no playful asides. New love in the face of lost love creates a sort of seriousness in itself. Joao, who in the past, had mostly kept to himself, took up muttering Portuguese at full volume, and followed up by trying to sing Brazilian songs over the Mexican music in the back kitchen. Jesus, who had previously practiced all of his newfound English cusswords with me, now took up a dialect of ancestral perfect Spanish, despite the fact that I speak a colloquial cuss-heavy pidgin-Oaxacan dialect. Michael, the self-appointed king of surprise crotch grabs and spatula handles up the butt, became suddenly serious, all business. He commanded the kitchen like a general leading his troops into war, and in this case, it wasn't a metaphor but a very serious sort of multinational standoff, with all the parties involved getting way too close to elaborately wasted. Like I said, I'm still impressed that nobody got stabbed.

We were busy that night. Busy like we hadn't been in weeks, and the business itself might have been the only thing that stood between a kitchen full of generally awkward culinary professionals, or angry, blood-thirsty assassins. Joao broke more plates than usual, and a few too many wine glasses hit the racks hard. Michael got loud with his calls for appetizers and desserts, as much to make himself heard over the clatter of plates and silverware as it was a subtle call for attention from the front. Both he and Joao alternated secret glances at the pass-through window, where Megan tacitly worked. When Megan brought back bus tubs, Joao hung his head and took them from her, only looking up as she turned away. As excited as I was for Michael that he might finally lose his virginity, I felt for Joao that he had lost his lover. Caught between the two, I still had a raw-meat-faced Oaxacan standing at my side, watching me cook everything wrong. "*Estas quemando tus cebollas*." He'd bark. "*Necesitas mas caldo*." He hung next to me all night, "*Que chingados, guey? Donde aprendistes a cocinar*?" Too many shots had turned him even surlier, and sloppier as well, but anything that went out wrong somehow ended up being my fault.

By the time that the rush had ended, without a single casualty, we were at the very least too exhausted to keep up the fight. Joao, unaccustomed to drinking, had started to run low, and bus tubs stacked up behind him. Jesus, despite his every effort, hadn't found a way to trip me up in perfect Spanish. After the last dessert plate went out, he bullied me off the line and took over cleanup so that I could help the broken-hearted Brazilian finish the dishes. Michael had lost some of his bravado. While we started the cleanup, he snuck out for a few minutes and returned with a case of Coronas for the kitchen. Once the line was clear, he busied himself out back, running through kitchen paperwork. Jesus threw his dirty apron in the rag bag and took a seat on the back porch, cradling his beer and gingerly pressing at the bruises on his face. Joao swept and mopped the kitchen as I ran the last of the glasses through the dishwasher and started the dishpit scrub down.

When we got out back, Jesus handed us each a beer, and the four of us sat around in a clump, nobody saying much. Joao sipped his beer, head hung, and his body crumpled forward on his stool. From the dining room, we could hear the sounds of Megan polishing the last of the glasses, only the faintest music still playing. She came out with the day's receipts and glanced over at us as she handed them to Michael. He took them, nodding, without looking up, as if he might betray his excitement. As she turned to walk back into the restaurant, Joao glanced up, his eyes glazing over. She caught it and stalled before stepping back in. Joao caught me watching. He sunk back into his beer, running his thumb around the lip of the bottle. When he raised it to drink again, he took a few long gulps, racing to the bottom. Jesus and I exchanged glances. Jesus shook his head, eyed his own beer, and swished the last few sips around. "Well," he said, "I'm going to get the fuck out of here." He downed the last of his beer and tossed it into the recycling bin with a crash. Michael looked up from his work, nodding. "*Mañana, guey.*"

Jesus pulled his jacket from the hook next to the door, and stepping out toward the parking lot, nodded at me and shrugged.

I nodded back. "*Te lo lavas*," I said.

He smiled. "I save the water for you to drink."

Joao watched him walk out, slugged back the rest of his beer, and straightened himself up. "*Vou para casa agora*," he said and stood, swaying.

Michael nodded without looking up.

"*Veja-o amanhã*," Joao said.

Michael nodded again.

Joao glanced over at me, waved goodbye, and shuffled out into the parking lot, stuffing his hands into his pockets.

Michael didn't look up from his page.

"That man is broken," I said.

Michael nodded. In all the time he had been sitting there, he hadn't written down a single thing, just stared at his page, columns of numbers in front of him, and the calculator sitting there, untouched.

I checked my beer. "So, uh, what do you say to a shot? Hit the Saloon? See if we can find those bastards?"

Michael looked up finally, glaring.

"Too soon?"

"I'm never going back to that shithole," he said.

"I'll buy?"

Megan came out the back door with her purse in her hands and her jacket over her arm. "Almost ready?" she asked.

Michael looked up, nodded solemnly, and glanced over at me. He closed his ledger and pushed his chair back as he stood up. "Not tonight, *güero*."

"I see."

I smiled at Megan, who stood there waiting. She smiled back. Her face flushed.

"Well, I guess I'll go see what I can't do about getting myself kicked out." I finished my beer and tossed it into the bin with another crash. Michael and Megan stood across the porch from each other, both waiting to lose a witness. "You guys stay out of trouble, okay?"

Megan giggled nervously.

"See you tomorrow, *Joto*?"

Michael nodded.

I pulled my hoodie from the hook and stepped out back, digging a cigarette out of the pocket. Through the vines that covered the patio, their voices were hushed, silhouettes moving behind the latticework, quietly coming together. As I moved off down the alley, the last of the lights went out in the kitchen, and the pair slipped out the back door.

Michael set the padlock and she stood near. She followed him to the passenger side door. He opened it for her, let her get settled, and closed it again. As he made his way back to the driver's side, he glanced up and down the alley. If he saw me, he didn't show it, and he pulled out, slinking off down the dark alley.

Fucking with the form

Doug lived across the street from my parents. He was a skinny fifteen-year-old with freckles and short reddish-blond hair. He was grounded most of the time, too smart for his own good and too lazy to hide it, so he got in trouble at school a lot. He talked fast and had a quick wit, and my only problem with him was that he didn't have an older brother to pester. An only child, his dad died in a boating accident when he was about five, so he had any toy he wanted, and always the expensive ones. The rest of the neighborhood kids took turns playing with his old toys. When he spotted me in the garage unbolting the front fairing, he walked over with his new airsoft pistol. Watching me work, he leaned against the front of the house and talked about some ridiculously expensive motorcycle that he wanted for his sixteenth birthday. As he talked, he aimed his pistol at anything that moved along the street.

"You're going to drive that thing to Seattle?"

I nodded, unscrewing another bracket from the frame.

"Really?" He pointed his pistol at Rosi. "Are you sure?"

"Yep."

He walked over, twisted the throttle a few times, and looked at it. "This thing is a piece of crap."

I brushed him away a few feet.

He pointed the pistol at me. "You're going to get yourself killed."

I laid the fairing on the concrete and pulled a hacksaw from my father's tool chest.

"What are you going to do with that?"

I stepped on one side of the fairing and braced the other side against my knee. "Customize." I set the blade against the piece and started sawing away most of the plastic.

"Don't you think they put that stuff there for a reason?" He poked at wires hanging from under the handlebars.

I kept hacking. "I think I hear your mom calling," I said.

"Mom won't be home until nine tonight. She's working."

"Great."

"This thing is fucking ugly, dude."

"I'm working on it."

"Not hard enough."

"Hey, you can fuck off any time you want to."

"Yeah, fine. Fuck you, too." He shot a pellet off at Rosi's windshield and backed down the driveway. "You gonna be here for a while?"

I nodded.

"I'll be back."

He crossed the street and left me alone with the pile of plastic scraps.

I spray painted the cowl flat black, duct-taped the broken windshield back together, and stuck an FKT sticker to it. The thing still seemed a little flimsy, but I dug through some of the crap in the garage, found a nice piece of metal mesh about the right size, pounded it flat, snipped it to fit, and ziptied it over the busted windshield. Maybe it didn't look pretty, but I was pretty sure it could deflect a rock, a junebug, a zombie or anything else that might get in the way.

Doug crossed the street as I was putting on the finishing touches. He checked out the paint job and nodded. "It's still a piece of shit," he said.

"Don't you have some homework to do?"

"Did it already."

"Maybe you can read ahead."

"I'm already getting an A."

"Great."

He stood by while I cranked down the fairing clips. "I brought you something," he said.

"A headache?"

"Here, man." He handed me a skull-and-crossbones patch. "I pulled it off my backpack. I figured if you're a pirate and all, you might need it. For your jacket."

"Thanks, man."

"Don't get killed."

He gave me a hug. I wasn't really expecting it, but maybe he was really worried. I guess he lost his dad years ago, so mortality wasn't really a foreign concept to him. That night, I dug through my trunk and found a spool of black thread and a thick needle. I drank a six pack of beer lying back in the rubber raft, stitching the *calavera* on the left shoulder of my leather jacket. And because I'm such a patriotic bastard, or maybe because I thought it might work as a disguise if I got pulled over along the way, I removed the American flag patch from my old Boy Scout uniform, and ironed it on to the other shoulder.

Dreamjar

The friendly, late-afternoon regulars had filtered out, and the early-evening kids were strolling in a few at a time, laughing already. I was a stranger to everyone except Jeff, the bartender, which was good for me. He kept my pint glass full, and he was busy enough that we didn't have to talk much. The bodies kept coming. They all smelled the same to me. They were the others, the zombies. The passive brain eaters, the social types that wanted to talk about exciting things and find out what I was all about. They wanted to tell me about what they did, find out what I did, and somehow combine these two useless subjects into some sort of scheme. A plan to friend each other on some online networking site, or meet up at a party later on, a reason to move and to shake. Some sort of intangible drinking game, meeting people to forget just after last call.

I kept my spiral open in front of me, trying to write a letter to Habibi, but *nothing* was coming out right. I was getting angry, blaming her for the shitpile I found myself wallowing in since she left. A half-dozen cocktails deep, my reflection started pissing me off. Every time I glanced up, he was there, glaring back at me, my own haggard, drunken blur of a face, shaking his head at me from the depths of the mirror behind the bar. One minute I was ignoring him, bent over my spiral, and the next, I was talking to the girl next to me, engaged in a conversation that made me a little uncomfortable.

"Have you ever seen a color in your dreams?" she asked.

Maybe I was single, but I didn't feel single yet. I half-expected Emira to walk in at any minute, find me talking to the blonde, and storm out in a fit of screaming jealousy.

She already stormed out, Sally.

She was leaned over the bar, leaning into me, some headless body sort of blonde, smiling like that, and trying her best to be profound.

Ask her if she knows her demons personally. Ask her if she's ever talked to them.

"Sure, doesn't everybody?" I said. Trying not to pay attention. Trying not to watch her silk blouse fall forward to reveal the early summer tanlines starting at the top of her breasts.

"No, not everybody." She swizzled her straw around her glass. It was red, vodka cran or something. "A lot of people don't even remember their dreams."

Ask her if she's named her monsters yet.

She leaned back. "A psychology professor once told me that if you remembered most of your dreams, your brain would be mush, but I don't believe that, because I remember most of mine."

I think her psychology professor was right.

"I remember a lot of my dreams," I said. "Too many, I think."

"Oh no, remembering them is important. I keep a journal of my dreams," she said. "Right next to my bed." She giggled. "So that I can write them down right after I wake up, unless I'm busy, you know?" she stirred her drink again and looked up at me with sex-kitten eyelashes batting. She was the kind of girl without a favorite color until she saw it on a Paris Hilton T-shirt, or maybe read it in a Brittney Spears interview. "Do you keep a dream journal?" Hell, she probably bought the dream journal with the Oprah stamp of approval.

I glanced down at my spiral and back to her. Pity for her felt horrid to me, but the tanlines were working for Cap'n Noskivvies. *She'll do,* he said. I smiled involuntarily. "I drink to forget my dreams," I said.

"Why would you want to do that?"

She's so precious.

"Not all dreams are happy, symbolic dream dictionary sorts of shit."

"But if you write them down, you really learn a lot about yourself."

I wondered what she might learn about me if she saw my dreams, the scary post-apocalyptic nightmares, the helldreams, the horror stories. "I dream when I sleep. These days, I'm trying to wake up."

"Oh, I can't imagine."

"Dreams aren't action, honey. Dreams are just dreams, and when I wake up, I wake up in the same damn shithole I fell asleep in. Living in my dreams just makes me tired."

"You should open yourself up, maybe. You're so closed off."

Oh, fuck yeah, open up.

As late as it was, the bar had mostly emptied out, and I might have been her last-chance booty call, the jackass with the spiral notebook, one too many whiskeys into my own dream journal. She didn't even look at me earlier, when they were all here, but hours later, after the rest had filtered out, maybe I was an option, maybe her only option. At the very least, I was still lucid. The last man standing when the lights came on again.

Jeff came over and offered us both a shot. Not the first I'd done with him, but with the blonde standing there, he made it seem that way.

"Do a shot with us?" he asked.

She nodded and smiled her nearly perfect teeth, breaking my heart.

He poured a round of shots, god only knew what was in them, but I nearly puked it all over the bar. He collected the glasses, took the last of my money left on the bar, and nodded his goodbye.

Me and the blonde made our way to the sidewalk out front.

"So where are you going now?" she asked.

Straight back to hell.

"Walking home," I said.

"You didn't drive?"

Go ahead, man, tell her about your murdercycle.

"Don't drive. I drink."

"Oh." She glanced down.

"Which way do you walk?" She glanced up the street and pulled hair back from her eyes, the breeze off the ocean making its way over the few blocks from the beach, just to catch a few rogue blonde strands.

Take her home, or take her here.

I felt like a giant looking down at her. I could have her. She could be mine, for a night at least. Hell, maybe she even lived nearby. Soft, perfume-smelling sheets with a high thread count, a dust ruffle, pillows, panties with lace, and the sun coming in through morning blinds to find us sleeping a foot apart, but naked.

What would she dream sleeping next to us?

Images of the apocalyptic aftermath flashed against the inside of my skull, waking up to search for bullet holes or the late night screams in my sleep, like hauling down a nightmare cocoon to smother the afterglow. We've tried this before, and it always ends badly. Mustn't set fire to paper souls. A spent condom or two crumpled beside the bed and the horror story for her afterward.

You're too hard on yourself.

I wanted her, if for no other reason than to use her like a scalpel, sever the limb, lose Habibi in a one-night stand, but she had those sad eyes and good, happy dreams. "You got a cell phone, honey?"

"Yeah."

"Let's call you a cab and get you home."

Fucking with the form II

The shop door was rolled up a few feet, the crackling blue light of a welder glimmering from inside. Mat squatted on a stool beside a new frame. After a few minutes, he noticed me sitting outside the garage door. He pulled off his visor and slid the door up a few feet. "I thought I smelled smoke." He pulled off his gloves, checked his weld, and laid the gloves over the frame. "What are you doing out here this time of night?"

"Pacing my cell."

"I figured you'd be gone by now."

"A few more days." I nodded at Rosinante. "She works. Now I'm gonna make her pretty."

He nodded and walked over to check her out.

"Nice," he said. "The tank sort of reminds me of the new Ducati tank." He petted her and looked her over.

"Need to make some renovations, streamline my escape pod. This is the dying field nag that's going to rocket me out of this hell."

"What the fuck are you talking about?"

"You got a grinder and a cutting wheel?"

He glanced back at the shop. "Yeah, come on in." He pulled a grinder from under his workbench. "You know how to change the disk?" He handed me a cutting wheel and a wrench.

I fumbled with it for half a minute, trying to look cool about it, but fuck if I knew how to use the stupid little wrench that changed the disk. Mat watched me without looking at me. He snatched it from me, pulled off the old buffing disk by hand and replaced it with the new cutting wheel.

He didn't have to say anything.

"I don't know. I just think this place can be a hell when you look at it right," I said.

"I forget how much you like to talk about stupid shit." He shook his head and ran an extension cord out to Rosinante.

I yanked off the side panels and checked to make sure that there were no wires in the way. "How far back do you think I can cut this?"

He squatted down next to Rosinante and looked over the frame, then leaned down and glanced under the back. "If you pull off the rest of the plastic back here, you could cut the frame all the way back to this weld here." He pulled a Sharpie from the shoulder of his coveralls and penned a line. "But I don't know how you'll attach your license plate."

"I'll zip tie it to the back or something."

"First big pothole, it'll go into your tire."

"I'll risk it." I gunned the grinder a few times. He handed me a set of safety glasses.

"Yeah, right, Yer a fuckin' badass, right?" He rolled his eyes at me.

"I can change my world anytime I want to. Make it the way that I want to," I said.

He leaned against the side of his panel van. "Anybody can."

"Sure, but they don't know it." I flicked the trigger a couple of times and kicked a rooster tail of sparks from Rosi's frame.

"How drunk are you?"

"Not drunk enough."

"Don't cut a finger off. You're not on our insurance."

He knelt down and took a look at the broken footpeg bracket.

"Hey man, most people get in accidents ten miles from home. I figure, I make it out of here, I got a decent shot at least."

He looked up from the footpeg bracket like I just woke him from a meditation, eyes light years away. "That's because most people never drive more than ten miles from their fuckin' homes." He shook his head.

He went back to the shop and left me to cut. I ground my edges clean, and in a few minutes, he was back with a handful of tools and a little finger-length chunk of quarter-inch steel with a hole drilled in one end. He knelt down next to Rosinante. In a few moments, he had pulled the bolts, set the hunk of steel against the frame, and bolted it to the bracket. He stood up and dusted himself off. "That ought to hold it."

The fifth rider

I pulled the tank and spray painted it flat black, but when I put it back on the bike, it still didn't look quite right. I dug through the trunks for model paint and spent the afternoon painting in racing stripes, painting them out, painting in flames, painting them out. Eventually, she had a long, chrome racing stripe, a big yellow star, Arabic cursive for pinstripes, and Sharpied in three tiny tombstones, for the number of times I'd raised her from the dead. I epoxied a waterproof clock to her tank. Bomb or time machine, either way, I was going to need to know time.

I took my helmet to the curb and spray painted it flat black. With the last of the model paint, I hand painted the crest of my helmet with a single, chrome warpaint stripe flowing into Habibi in Arabic cursive.

I splurged on a brand-new pair of 501s and spent a day shrinking them. I tossed them in the sink, poured a few pots of boiling water over them. I washed them with my old jeans. I took a hot bath in them reading my stolen copy of Quixote. I swam through a warm, sunlit swimming pool in them. I waded into a moonlit ocean in them. I washed them and dried them and then they fit okay.

I had a week left until the tags ran out and barely enough money to make it to San Francisco, let alone the fees to re-register Rosinante. I had the brakepads, but the clock was already ticking, and I figured if I didn't get on the road soon, I wasn't going to.

I packed my old saddlebags. Boots, an extra pair of jeans. A couple of Clean t-shirts, spare socks, and a couple of books. My sketchpad, some colored pencils. I packed an extra sweater, the new front brakepads, a ratchet handle and a handful of useful heads. A couple screwdrivers, two adjustable wrenches, A can of WD40, some carb cleaner, a roll of duct tape, a fistful of zip ties, of varying sizes.

I tucked a hoodie and some gloves into my backpack. A big bottle of water, a little water bottle full of lamp oil, my rope and wicks wrapped in a fire rag, stuffed down in the bottom. I had a disposable drug store camera, a pen, a spiral notebook, and the little leather journal Michael and Monica gave me as a going away gift. I bungeed it all to the backseat.

Rosinante looked miserable all loaded up, but I said I was going to be on the road by noon, and the clock on Rosi's tank said two. Everybody was over me saying that I was about to take off, and the goodbyes had all been doubled. *The saddlebags are too much resistance.* Figuring that I'd be in Portland within the week, I jettisoned the bags and packed them in a box, with the Amazons for a shipping address. I figured I could cruise California easy in sneakers and a t-shirt, the rest I would fix just before I got there. Ready for my triumphant march into her waiting arms.

Whoever was left gave another round of hugs. I zipped up my jacket, nodding and smiling. I had hoped to do a quick victory lap through town before I left, but time was running short. I turned the key and pushed the button. Rosinante started right up. There was a murmer of approval, and I think some money changed hands between the kids. I backed her down the driveway, revving her engine to blow out a few of the cobwebs. I zipped up the sleeves of my jacket, and checked my helmet strap.

In all my armor, my leather jacket and brand new blue jeans, my helmet, bristling crest emblazoned, I rode the first quarter mile proud. As a man about to embark on a journey, I was endless space dust, waiting to form. I was free. For at least today, I was free. I pulled into the gas station on the corner and rolled up to the pump, already squinting like some gunslinger TV rerun. I took off my helmet and carried it in with me to the register, pulling a decent wad of gas money out of my pocket, ready to pay the first ten dollar ding.

I was already immortal, the whole ride was a victory lap. In years past, I'd done the drive in seventeen hours. At a city a day, all the important stops, I figured I could be back in her arms in about a week. It was as good as done. I hung my helmet on the handlebars, and unzipped my jacket; like the last block had been a hard ride, and I just needed the air. I picked the high grade, for the octane boost, and put the key into the gascap. When I flipped it up, it banged against the clock casing. I tried to look cool about it, but I had to slide the fuel nozzle in sideways to get the gas to pump.

Holy hellfire

In third gear at nine grand, Rosinante pulled ninety miles per hour easy. That new Yoshi exhaust pipe was like a drill in my skull. At that speed, the wind was tearing my helmet off, tugging at my jacket zipper, choking me from behind in the parachute of my sweatshirt hood. Ninety miles an hour and I never took it above third. This was not the work of a dying field nag. Suddenly, the EX meant something. Her purr turned to an unflinching roar. It was all I could do to cling tighter to Rosi's back as she barreled headlong into the center of my least favorite city. I was sorry that I ever doubted her.

The last few miles of freeway were tar-stitched fissures and seams in the sun-baked concrete, potholes filled with asphalt that rattled the frame like a drumbeat, painfully steady. By the time I pulled off the freeway, I was already beat to shit. Only two hours into a thirteen-hundred-mile ride, and I could feel the road straight into my bones. My shoulders knotted and torqued around the gravel in my neck, a haphazard cable of sinew and ligaments petrified beneath my skin. At the off-ramp, I sat up, but it hurt worse to ride that way.

I found Geoff and Karen’s place easily. The place was fenced off, with a big green metal gate. I rolled Rosinante up to the curb, climbed off into a stretch, and pulled off my helmet. I rang the bell but there was no answer the first time. When I rang it the second time, Karen called from the yard. “Aaron?”

“Yup.”

She slid the gate open a few feet and came out to hug me. “You made it.” She sounded surprised.

“The beast lives.”

She looked at Rosinante. “Is that Q’s old bike?”

I nodded.

“The one that was in front of the Lair for all those years?”

"The same."

"That thing runs?"

"Apparently."

"And you're going to try to drive it all the way to Seattle?"

"Yeah."

"You're crazy," she said.

"We'll see."

"Well come in." She slid the gate open a little farther so that I could push Rosi into the courtyard. "Geoff's in the office, on the phone."

I first met Geoff and Karen while I was working with the fire troupe in Seattle. They were two of the original thirteen members. When the troupe began to grow, they sold Geoff's house in Seattle and moved to Los Angeles to be closer to his business and to start another franchise troupe. They did gigs all over California, and called Emira and I up to help every once in a while. I didn't get to perform with them much, though. I spin a meteor. It's twelve feet of rope with wicks at either end. Big fire, and not easy to pull off in a little bar or nightclub somewhere. Those days, most of the performances were fire eating, dancing with fans, or couples work. Not much room for a guy who twirls a rope around. They were glad to see me, at least. Geoff set up a couple of ouzo shots for us. I'm one of the few people he knows who will drink it with him, and we sat around the kitchen table sipping the licorice liqueur, catching up on the past few months.

They were just getting ready to go out for the evening, to meet Geoff's kid sister Sarah at a local art opening. It was a few blocks away but we couldn't decide if we wanted to go out for drinks first, so we strolled around the neighborhood a few times before settling on free wine or whatever we could find at the opening.

The art opening itself was *nothing* spectacular. Someone took a bunch of panoramic photos of palm trees and cityscapes, blew them up to poster size, and lined the walls with them. Anybody else with a disposable camera might have done the same. We've replaced the pastoral landscapes with images of the scenes outside our own doors. Or maybe the scenes outside our doors are all that remain. The hills and fields have all but vanished in streets lined with transplanted trees, sidewalks, and power lines. I take small comfort in the idea that soon I'll be out of hell and moving into the green margins of Highway 101.

The gallery was first story on the street-side second floor of the building, with a set of stairs at the rear heading down into a paved yard. An aluminum streamline trailer rested against one fence with an enormous pink flamingo strapped to the side and a folding table set out in front of it. Bodies milled about the yard getting drunk on cheap wine.

Geoff and Karen talked with the artists who arranged the show. I squeezed in to get us a few plastic cups of Chianti. We stood around in the yard, too sober to really engage yet.

Sarah showed up after the second cup. She stood at the top of the stairs searching the crowd for Geoff and Karen. She wore a big knit cap and a giant sweater, but I recognized her right away. Geoff waved at her, and she made her way down the stairs, into the yard.

I met her once, years ago. She camped with us at a big fire event in the desert. She stayed in a motorhome with Geoff and Karen. I had a tent a ways off with the rest of the fire troupe. A few times we talked, but a couple of days in, her boyfriend arrived. He was the son of a Peruvian holy man. It seemed a bad idea to try and get in the middle of that. Besides, he seemed like a nice guy.

She hugged Geoff and Karen and smiled at me. "Haven't seen you in years."

"Been busy."

She hugged me. It was sort of unexpected. I hugged her back, a little awkward.

"How was your drive?"

"Not bad so far," I said.

"Geoff tells me that you're driving all the way to Washington."

"Yep."

"Well, you showed up just in time, at least," Sarah said.

"In time for what?"

"We're thinking about going up to the cabin for a few days."

"What's this cabin?"

"You'll love it. You have to go." She smiled.

"We're kidnapping you," Geoff said. "We won't take no for an answer."

"I have to get to back to Habibi," I said.

"C'mon, Cap'n, you're on an adventure." Geoff laughed and slapped me on the back. "Besides, it's just a couple days."

"Alright, well, at least send her a ransom note or something."

When we got back to Geoff and Karen's place, they left me on the front porch. I lit a cigarette and paced to stretch my legs a little more. Only a couple of hours on the road, even a couple of hours to rest, but I was still feeling it. Right beside the front walkway there was a fountain gurgling down a stack of rocks into a koi pond. The front drive was a fenced garden surrounding the pond. Banana palms and ferns grew out of a washed gravel driveway. It was an untouched realm of tranquility fenced into the center of an otherwise sun-decayed stretch of asphalt and sickly queen palms that composed most of Hell-A. The sound of the water was sublime to my ringing ears. Rosinante rested beside a patch of lush, tropical grasses. If ever there was a more hospitable stable for a burnout nag, I couldn't imagine it. She rested. She earned it.

For a few moments, it seemed as if the city slept. The thin wash of traffic was faint and shore-like under the calls of night birds. Somewhere, a sprinkler worked its midnight magic on a perpetually green lawn. The ringing in my ears subsided some, and the rocks in my neck and shoulders softened back to flesh. Somehow, the city wasn't so bad lost in the Hollywood Hills. Everything outside that fence might be burning in hellfire, but I wouldn't know because the porch was so damn serene after the lashing I took getting there. A haze descended on the city, casting the sunburnt patina in impressionist light. I could spend a day or two there, I guess. Soak up some of the silence.

But from the east, the still air was shredded by a police siren.

Captivity

Time moves differently in a place with no clocks. No phones, no traffic, no TV. Rocks, dirt, chaparral, hawks, lizards, bugs, and the sun rolling slow across a stretch of eternal blue. For a few hours, we listened to a frog. He croaked steadily through the afternoon. Geoff and Karen napped inside. I sat in the shade of an *uña de gato*, reading. Sarah drifted around the pool on an air mattress, sipping a drink and reading in a little pair of white panties and a big floppy sun hat. After a while, she set her book, drink, and hat on the edge of the pool and slid off into the water. She shimmered beneath the surface, pale skin against the dark concrete bottom, and when she rose again, it was in the corner beneath the *uña de gato*. Her hair was liquid as she leaned against the edge of the pool beside me. Her skin was soft and pale, and her shoulders were already pink. "Getting toasty?" I asked.

"Cream cheese," she said.

"Okay," I said, and nodded like I understood.

"That's what Geoff and I used to call a fart."

"Oh."

The frog croaked again.

"See," she said.

"Oh, I get it." I pulled out a cigarette and lit it. "Seems a funny place for a frog, out in the middle of the desert," I said.

"They come up to the pool to find a mate," she said. "I always feel bad when we empty the pool."

"I guess this must be a pretty swank mating ground, the private pool."

"Except it never lasts." She rested her chin on her hands. Droplets ran from her hairline down her cheek. "How's your book?"

"Pretty good."

"You've hardly moved."

"Almost fifty pages." I shrugged. "I've been all over the place in the past two hours."

She smiled. "You like to read a lot?"

"Whenever I can."

"Me too." She wiped a drop from her eyebrow and glanced down at her chest. She pressed her fingers against her skin and let it go to see how much sun she had gotten. "What do you like to read?" she asked.

"Adventure stories."

She nodded, tilted her head, and looked at me. "They make me want to go have an adventure," she said.

I nodded. "Me, too."

The frog croaked again.

"Cream cheese," I said.

She smiled.

Geoff cracked the bottle of ouzo and poured a couple of shots for us. Karen started washing vegetables for dinner and absolutely refused to let me pour her a drink. "You pour mostly alcohol," she told me. Geoff and I did our shots and he poured two more.

After a couple of shots, Geoff dropped his trunks in the middle of the living room and ran out toward the pool buck-ass naked. He hopped off a rock overhanging the pool and splashed down. The whole lot of them are nudists. "You should try it," he hollered. "Where else can you go swimming naked before dinner?" I did another shot of ouzo and made Karen cover her eyes while I stripped and took the plunge. I came back to the surface sputtering and clawing for the edge. Geoff laughed. "You have to keep your legs closed when you hit."

Geoff swam a few laps while I tread water at the far corner of the pool. Maybe he was used to swimming around naked in the evening, but it was going to take some practice for me. After a few minutes, he hopped out of the pool, shook off some water, and walked into the Cabin. He crossed into the kitchen, grabbed the bottle of ouzo and the shot glasses, kissed Karen, and brought the bottle out to the edge of the pool. "Another Shot?" but he was already pouring them. I wanted a shot, but he was crouched down next to the edge of the pool, pouring the shots, and I wasn't sure if I wanted the shot bad enough to get a closer look at his junk. He set the bottle on the edge of the pool and hopped back in, holding the full glasses above his head.

"So you and Emira must be getting pretty serious," he said, wading over towards me.

I nodded, not really sure what to tell him. I threw back the ouzo shot and winced.

"I hate to say it, but Karen and I really weren't sure how long you guys were going to last."

"That makes a few of us." I offered him the glass for a refill.

"Well it's nice to see, anyway. So many of our friends have broken up over the past few years, it's good to see a couple getting a few years on together."

I thought back over the time that he had known about me and Emira, the number of breakups that he'd never heard about. Hell, we were on and off about every three weeks for nearly two years. After a while, we just stopped telling people about the drama because they stopped listening. The most recent breakup was just one of the many that I never bothered to tell anyone about.

"Well you and Karen seem pretty happy," I said.

He glanced back into the kitchen at his wife. They'd been together for nearly a decade, and seemed pretty solid.

"Yeah," he said. "We're thinking about having a baby soon."

"That's great." I tried to imagine Habibi and I getting to that point, but after a few months apart, even the idea of living together again seemed ridiculous.

"Yeah, except we don't want to have it here," he said.

"Yeah, I hate L.A." I said.

He shrugged. "Not just L.A." he poured himself another shot and offered me the bottle. "Karen and I don't want to raise a child in this country." He downed his shot and gazed off over the boulders overlooking the city below. "It's getting hard on the soul."

"It's been that way for years." I said. "You were raised here. Karen was raised here. I was raised here. Somehow we turned out alright."

He smiled and laughed nervously.

"Okay, you and Karen turned out alright."

He chuckled again, easier this time. "With the wars, the occupation of the middle east and the way our government is handling its foreign policy, it's only a matter of time before the war comes back to us."

"Sure, but that's always been a risk."

He nodded. "We don't want to raise our child in an atmosphere of fear and oppression."

There was a time when others might have said that of foreign countries. "I don't know, you take a chance anywhere, really."

"Yeah, but the way things are going with the United States, it just seems like the whole country took a turn for the worse a few years back, and it doesn't seem to be getting any better."

I nodded. I guess spending the past few months drinking, and worrying about Habibi, I just wasn't paying much attention to the news. I used falling out of love as an excuse to ignore all sorts of things. For whatever reason, the thought occurred to me that I probably hadn't called my mother enough recently, either.

"We just want to find a space for ourselves, somewhere that we can raise a family; someplace safe."

I glanced past him to the cabin, saw Karen and Sarah moving around in the kitchen, prepping vegetables for dinner. Sarah stopped what she was doing, laughed at something Karen said, and turned to look at me, the smile lingering just before she looked away. "You want to make a home," I said.

He nodded, followed my glance, and leaning against the edge of the pool, smiled in at his wife and sister, framed by the kitchen windows. "Exactly," he said. "Home." He picked up the bottle from the rock beside the pool, refilled both our glasses and offered his for a toast. "To home," he said.

"Harumph," I said, and we drank.

The dreaming

Sarah and I woke up at the same time. I sat up to find her tangled in her sheets, facing me, with a contented smile and sleepy eyes. I rubbed my face and glanced around the cabin like I was surprised to be back. "How did you sleep?" I asked.

"I dreamt that we were children in some festival in China," she said.

"Were we wearing red paper hats?" I asked.

She smiled. "Yes, and making things out of red paper."

"Was there a lot of gold leaf on the paper?"

She nodded and nestled further into her pillow.

"Yep, that was it," I said. I laid back and stared up at the ceiling. "Well, that's creepy enough."

She threw a pillow at me.

"I just mean that I'm rarely in the same dream with someone else and remember it."

"Creepy makes it sound bad." She sat up at the edge of the bed and stretched. She was in a pair of boxer shorts and an old wife-beater T-shirt. The fabric of the shirt was futile, revealing more than enough of her figure. Despite the fact that she was a couple of years older than me, there was something innocent and childlike about her pert breasts and pale skin. "Want to go for a swim?" she asked.

"What the hell." I jumped up, stuffed my sheets and comforter back into the corner, and stretched with my back to her.

"I remember that crow," she said, apparently about my tattoo.

"Yeah?"

"You painted it on the back of my hand the first time we met. It didn't wash off for days." She inspected the back of her right hand like it might still be there.

"I got a thing for those birds," I said.

She folded her comforter and stacked the pillows at the edge of the bed. "I know." It made perfect sense that she might. "In a few dreams, you've had a pet crow that sits on your shoulder. You kept telling me that you could fly when no one was looking."

"Did the crow talk?"

"I don't think so," she said. "It just sat there."

"Did he tell you his name?"

"Oh, I don't know, it was just a crow."

Sarah came out onto the patio with a couple of bottles, a small plastic dish, and some sort of a paint brush. She took a seat next to me and set her fixings in front of her. "How is the book?" she asked.

"Good." I placed the bookmark in the center and folded it in my lap.

"I'm going to bleach my hair," she said, setting up the bleach kit. After watching her struggle for a few minutes, I stepped up behind her, took the brush, and worked the bleach into a lock of her hair. I took a piece of foil from the table, gently wrapped the bleached lock, and combed out another one to paint.

"You've done this before?"

I nodded. "Years ago, I used to bleach my bangs with a girl I knew. She had long platinum dreadlocks that needed touch-ups every once in a while, and most of the time, I'd help her. If I was drunk enough, I'd bleach my bangs out too."

"I can't imagine you with blonde hair."

"We quit talking once Habibi and I got together. Habibi wasn't much on me having a lot of other girls in my life."

"Yeah. Jaime is pretty jealous, too." She glanced down at her hands and tried not to move too much.

"Always seemed like it caused more problems than it cured." I shrugged.

She settled back in her seat and sighed.

"I'm just not sure where we're going," she said.

"Who is sure?" I wrapped another lock of hair in foil and combed out the next. After a few, she seemed to relax even more and laid her head back on the chair. I continued to comb out locks, baste them, and wrap them in foil. After just a few minutes, she had a mane of crumpled aluminum dreadlocks and sat topless in her chair, sunbathing. My metal serpent Medusa, this immortal Circe, bleach-blonde seductress. And yet, she wasn't. Really, she was just a girl, and I was just a guy, and the whole thing was a lot simpler than it seemed, sitting around half-naked on a sunny porch. I was petrified by her presence, and I was an entirely willing captive.

After a few minutes of silence, she sighed, sat up, and inspected my hair. I tried not to stare at her breasts as she leaned forward to run her fingers through my hair. She stood without letting go and walked around behind me, still running her fingers through my hair, pulling out a few choice strands. She held my head back against her tummy, and still holding a few locks, reached for the dish of bleach. "I'll bet you look cute with a couple of highlights," she said. I wasn't in a position to argue. "Just a few strands," she said, "like your warpaint." Holding my head firmly against her chest, she painted in an indelible stripe. "So that everyone will know that you are on a quest."

"Tell me what you think of these photos," she said, and opened a scrapbook in front of me. She leaned back in her chair and watched me.

The photos were of a street somewhere. Wide open space to one side, and a thicket of bushes and trees to the other. Some of the photos looked in on the thicket. At first, they seemed pastoral, somewhat bland, forest scenes. As the photos went on, they became a little more human. Deep in the tangles of blackberry bushes there were bits of cloth, an old tire, the sheen of black plastic trash bags. The pretty forest was rotting at the roots.

"It looks like a dumping ground," I said.

Sarah didn't flinch. "But how does it make you feel?"

"I mean, it looks really pretty, but then there's all this trash here." As I looked at it, it started to make me feel a little bit sick. "The composition is nice and everything, but the place itself gives me the creeps." I looked at a picture with the most trash in it. The way the tires lay, and the old clothes tangled in the bushes made it look like a bed of some sort, a squatter's place, maybe. "I don't much like the place," I told her.

She leaned forward and closed the book. "You're sensitive, aren't you?" She made it sound so gay.

"I dream hard, that's all. Sometimes I can't tell what's real."

"You're right," she said. "The photos are of a bad place." She scooted her chair back and stood. "I'm going to make another drink. Would you like one?"

I drained the rest of my glass. I got the feeling like we were negotiating for something. "Yes," I said.

She took my glass and made us both drinks. "Let's sit on the patio," she said.

We moved to the patio. I kept quiet and gave her space to speak. She sipped her cocktail and sat staring out over the valley below, thinking about something. When she spoke, she didn't look at me. "When I was fourteen, I decided to run away from home, so I packed some things into a duffel bag and climbed out my bedroom window."

I lit a cigarette and leaned back in my chair.

"I was hitchhiking a few blocks away from the house when a car pulled over. He picked me up and drove to the freeway." She wouldn't make eye contact. My heart sank slowly.

"He turned out to be a copycat Green River Killer. You remember the Green River Killer, right?"

I nodded.

"So this guy drove me out to a road just off the freeway. It was a place that the Green River Killer dumped a few bodies." She looked at the pool. "I remember him choking me, and I left my body for a while. I remember watching the police pull up behind his car. I remember watching the flashlights along the gravel up to the driver's side door. That was when the police started yelling at him. They took him out of the car. I decided that I wanted to live, so I went back into my body." She said it so plainly, there was *nothing* else to believe.

"Did they arrest him?"

"Yeah, but he was never convicted." She glanced down.

I was angry.

"I went back there to take pictures, and I got myself in trouble." She sat forward. "I'm sorry, could I smoke one of your cigarettes?"

I pulled one out for her. She looked it over. "I haven't smoked for three years." She placed the cigarette to her lips. "I went to see a psychic."

I lit her cigarette. She inhaled deeply and nodded. "She said that I had four spirits following me. They were four girls who died there. They followed me because they saw me die, and saw me live again. They were drawn to the power of my will." She blew at the ember and flicked the ash away. "The psychic cleared me of the four ghosts, and I've had to think on it." She leaned back in her chair. "I want to go plant flowers there, but the psychic told me that I can never go back. She said that I would pick up more ghosts next time, maybe some that she couldn't clear away." She inhaled hard, and spoke through a veil of smoke. "But I'd like to find places like it, and plant wildflowers there, for the dead."

I've heard that the story of the world is the story of a mad god. I've heard that it's the story of the death of the Earth mother. I've heard that it's a collection of random events that so happen to coincide with a lot of other random events, and that it's just luck that we're all walking around here wondering why we're all walking around here wondering. I've heard a lot of things. Maybe everybody's got their own story of the world; a personal genesis myth, so to speak. I always sort of thought of it in terms of cowboys and angels.

Angel falls to earth one day, and that's where the cowboy wakes up. He doesn't know how he got there, and he doesn't really have to, because he's a cowboy, and every day is gonna end up the same anyway. But there she is, this angel. Maybe she's got a busted wing. Hell, maybe he's got a busted wing for that matter. She's all righteous, and he just is. Or maybe he's all righteous, and she just is. But that's the beauty and the beast of it. And they gotta get through this desert somehow. Really, that's as far as I got with the thing. They're strolling through the desert. Hell, let's say they're arm in arm, even. Yeah, now that's pleasant.

The nice thing about a personal mythology is that it suffices to answer my own questions about the nature of the world in general. The hard part of it is that it's like seeing dragons in the clouds. No two people see the same shapes. Sure, sometimes you can find a bunny or something, clowns make balloon animals out of that, but try picking out something hard, like Elvis on a motorcycle or whatever. Cloud watching is the hobby of loners. It is a pastime of dreamers. Sometimes, it's the only way to lose the thoughts I wish I didn't have.

I spent the afternoon with a book open in my lap, but I wasn't getting much reading done. The bastard got away. That part was killing me. He tried to kill her, and then he walked away. They pegged her for a prostitute and let him ride. There were no rogue cops to shoot him dead on the spot, no cunning TV lawyers to put him away for life. There was a half-assed attempt at justice that ended in her surrender. A part of me wanted to go hunting.

As the sun started dropping, Sarah put on her clothes again and pulled a chair up next to me. "Not reading much," she said. The sun set the mountains ablaze behind her. The pink clouds warmed the rocks. Everything seemed alive, bathed in soft pastels and shades of some unpainted Maxfield Parish scene.

"Too high." I smiled.

She nodded. "It's a lot to process." She smiled back. "Sorry to drop it on you."

I nodded.

I wanted to reach out into the sky and reshape the clouds, show her what I saw. I wanted to sculpt a set of sideburns on that fluffy bunny cloud, and set a couple of cumulus wheels to spinning so that she'd know exactly where I was coming from. Better yet, I would have liked to sweep my hand across the sky, brushing away the distant clouds, leaving her a crystal clear blue horizon, to do whatever she wanted with it.

Under the circumstances, about all I could do was offer her my arm and walk with her a while.

The ghost

Geoff and I hiked up the drive until we reached the top. From there we could see the entire valley below, hash marks of highways leading into clusters of stucco and palm trees. The fountains caught the late afternoon light as the shadows began to creep across the valley floor. He told me about the crazy old guy building patios all around his cabin and pointed it out, crammed up into the armpit of the hill. He pointed to a spot where he and his dad saw an eagle when he was a kid.

We left the road and carved a track up the side of the hill, watching the bushes and rocks for snakes. When we got to the top of the hill he pointed down at the canyon. "A fire burned this whole hillside ten years ago. It got close to burning the cabins." He pointed at a cluster of palm trees deep at the end of the canyon, the cliffs swept up behind it into craggy dried falls. "The bases of those palms never see the sunlight. Their trunks are still burnt. A few died, but the rest came back."

"What's down there?"

"Palm trees, mostly." He took a swig of water and passed the bottle to me. "And the ghost."

"Ghost?" *Now we're getting somewhere.* "What is the ghost?"

"A friend of ours was up here a while back, walking around down there. He's a mountaineer, so he'd go off walking for days. He ended up down there and then he said he felt like he was being stalked by something."

"Like an animal?"

"No. Like something evil."

"Did he see anything?"

"He just felt it stalking him." Geoff took another drink and screwed the cap back on the bottle. "Must've scared him pretty bad, though. He ran all the way back to the cabin."

"How do we get down there?"

"You have to hike all the way up from the little spring that we were at earlier."

I peered over the cliff face. The bottom of the canyon was shrouded in shadow. By the time that we got to the spring, it would already be dark. "Can we go tomorrow?"

"We were planning on taking off early to beat the traffic back into the city. Sounds like Sarah is going to stay another night though. If you really want to hike up there, Sarah could use some help cleaning up the cabin. I'm sure she wouldn't mind the company."

Burn

I don't know, but I'm told that fire spinning began centuries ago as a form of inter-island communication. Some say that the poi started in New Zealand; others have told me that it's the knife burning from the Samoans. I always liked that; the idea that islands were calling each other by way of some fire flinging semaphore. How it started, I don't care. Wherever the fire phone-a-friend option began, it was somewhere in the Pacific Ocean, in the middle of the ring of fire.

My preferred burn is the meteor, a ten foot length of rope with wicks at either end. Started as a Buddhist meditation, somewhere in Japan, it's the feminine form of the kung fu fighting weapon, the "claw". Originally, the Buddhists spun twin bowls of water at either end of the rope for three years, or until they were able to spin them without spilling a drop.

The first time I spun fire, I was half crocked on a beach in Seattle, playing with the fire troupe after a month of spinning the rope in my friends' backyard. Fuck the Buddhist bowls, man. We got Kevlar wicks, these days, and I can afford to burn some hair off.

Geoff picked a spot up the hill. The clearing listed northeast, mostly gravel with a few sparse chunks of red rock, fairly weather worn, and decently smooth surfaces to stumble on. I knew Geoff was close to his burn spot because he finally looked down, and started brushing the little chunks of stone and dried sage detritus out of the way. He nodded at me. I set down the bucket in the bottleneck before the downhill path, a few feet away from the bushes.

Geoff took his satchel off his shoulder, and pulled his water bottle from the sidepocket. He took a sip and eyed the valley floor spread out below us. The sun was just touching the tops of the hills to the west, and the shadow crept towards us. Below, in the valley, lights were becoming visible. Another evening awakening and the city below, dressed in neon and colored lights glimmering in the magic hour. From where we stood, we could see the cabin, Karen and Sarah turning on the kitchen lights, and the porch light catching the swimming pool, shimmering gossamer.

He pulled a black bundle from his fire bag. Setting it on the ground beside him, he folded back the corners of his fire rag to reveal his chains coiled around a small pair of Kevlar wicks. He stretched them out, slipped his fingers through the handles and let them hang before him. "It's been a while," he said, and stretched his arms out, pulling one across his chest, and then the other. "We haven't been spinning as much these days."

"I thought you guys were working with that troupe?"

He shrugged. "Every once in a while we do a show." He spun a couple of times, absentmindedly ran through a few combinations like a habit.

When I popped the lid on the fuel canister, he smiled and nodded, and held the chains together, setting the wicks into the fuel, and dangling the chains over the side of the canister. Back when we were doing this sort of thing on a weekly basis, performances on the weekends, practices on Tuesdays, this sort of moment came with a lot of chatter. People checked their entrances, double checked their fire safety, last minute peeks into the mirror to inspect their makeup or costume. We got nervous before lit performances, watched the crowd from offstage, listened to the music for cues, nodded to the beat and prepared. But two guys standing on a hill in the middle of the desert, there wasn't much to prepare. There was a nostalgic reverence in the fueling process.

Aside from a few rogue burns on the beach, I hadn't burned much in the past year. I worked too much, and without a regular gig, I had grown lazy in my practice sessions. Pyromancing, however, is one of those things that, if practiced enough, etches itself into your muscle memory. I pulled the knotted coil of rope from my satchel, and unwinding it, dropped the wicks into the can of fuel.

Geoff continued to stretch out, twisting his arms and legs into funny positions. He and Karen were into yoga, and that sorta thing, so a couple of his stretches probably had some Hindi name. I dug into my satchel for my gloves, found a cigarette and my lighter, and hunkered down a few feet away from the fuel bucket.

"So how far do you think you'll make it?" he said, like he was in on the betting pool with the neighborhood kids, and he was checking odds.

I glanced out at the puddle of lights in the valley, trying to pick out veins of street lamps and the highway beyond. "I don't know, Geoff. Maybe all the way."

He smiled. "I can't believe that motorcycle is still running. It was out in front of the Lair for years before you got it."

"Yeah."

"Have you thought about just flying up there?"

I looked at Geoff.

He smiled and shrugged.

"Wanna burn something." I said.

He nodded.

He twisted his fingers into the handles of his poi, and lifted the wicks from the bucket. The fuel dribbled off into the bucket, and when it slowed, he pulled the chains a few feet away and spun off the excess fuel. He rolled his head, and smiled, nodding his head. I pulled on my gloves, flicked my lighter, and cradling the flame in a leather clad palm, offered him a light.

Geoff spins clean, clinical. His secret name is Fusion, and he works his wicks like particles orbiting a nucleus. A mostly symmetrical pattern of flames whirling fast around muscle-memory-solid moves. He is the doctor. The fire is his patient. He knows it like a man who has studied it for decades. He has rhythm, and like the subtle nuances of a tea ceremony, he expresses himself in the slightest gesture, a glad flick of the wrist. A surprise drop and twist into some coy behind the back set of metered triples that bounce and flicker like an insect folding its flaming wings to settle on a branch. The chains obey his every suggestion, natural extensions, an expression of his secret self.

As the flames begin to sputter, he pulls his spin in, slows, and glances outside his burn sphere long enough to find me, crouched a few feet off, rope hung around my neck, and a couple feet of charred nylon cord twisted up in each fist, looking more like a desert hunter than a fire dancer. Geoff approaches slow, savoring the last flickering moments, and leaning forward, the wicks float up, pausing only long enough to pass the flame.

Closed, the rope folded in two, and wicks met, the meteor's opening moments are every bit like its namesake. A single white hot ball of fire swinging pendulous at first, and then up, and around uncertainly, a thing gloriously united by the sound of the white gas flame streaking around the chewy chocolaty center of my spin circle. I don't have Fusion's perfect grace, none of his practiced moves, and for the first few orbits, it might look like I'm about to fling that thing off into some sort of low orbit, careening down to the center of the dark canyon below to reignite the fire that charred the canyon years ago. But once it's open, it is the yin and yang, twin centers spiraling eternally away from each other, the one, following the other, tangling lines until they wind up, to bounce away again. Away, and around again. I spin like a drunken puppetmaster, chasing two flickering crepe goldfish in their mating dance, paper flames, and things that fade away. They chase each other around my legs, above my head, in circles around my body, dancing toward each other, and dancing away. Until, at long last, they come back together, dance slow and close for a while, manicuring the mutual burn, and eventually, sputter out as one quick smoking-hot loss of momentum. I don't spin fire, so much as write love poetry in open flames. A long distance phone call to a long distant love.

The ghost II

I woke up to a strong certainty that I was not where I belonged. More than just waking from a dream, it was knowing, without a doubt, that the mountain cabin was not real, or that I was merely a ghost myself, haunting it like a memory. Sarah sat up in her own bed, rubbed her eyes, and blinked at me. “Woah,” she said.

I looked around at the cabin. It seemed real enough. Sarah seemed real. We stared at each other. “Where were we last night?” I asked.

She shook her head and leaned forward, squinting back into her subconscious. “It was--” she looked up at me, looked through me. “It was dark, underground, or a prison, maybe.” She threw her feet over the edge of the bed, planting them on the tile floor. “You were there, or somebody like you, but darker.” She just stared at me. “He was angry, and violent. He kept tearing at the walls, trying to escape.” She ran her fingers through her hair and looked out the window, bracing herself with the light. “It was so dark.”

I watched her, feeling like I should apologize for something, although I couldn’t remember exactly what. This is the sort of dreaming that made me nervous, but curious, too. Whatever she saw, I couldn’t see it, the wasteland dreams, the apocalyptic end-time dreams.

She stood and smiled nervously. Something had changed between us. There was a sort of fear in her eyes. “The crow was there,” she said.

“He was?”

She smiled again, but this time a little more relaxed. “He told me not to worry.” Then she relaxed entirely, as if shedding the dream entirely, and standing solidly in the cabin. “Isn’t that funny?" she said. "A talking crow." She pulled the quilt up over the bed and stretching, dismissed the whole thing.

Geoff and Karen packed the car before getting ready to go down to the stream. Sarah moved her truck so that they could get ready to leave, and packed a cooler with snacks and drinks. In spite of the fact that she'd seemed to have shaken off the dream, she also kept her eye on me. Every time I turned around, she was watching me, maybe trying to reconcile the difference between the man that she'd seen in the dreams, and the mostly harmless drunk sitting next to her pool, reading and drinking a vodka cranberry for breakfast.

On the walk down to the stream she walked beside me, but quietly. I carried the cooler, and we ambled along awkwardly, following Geoff and Karen; a default couple, trying to forget an uncomfortable moment. I tried to tell myself that it wasn't what I thought. Maybe she was embarrassed about telling me about the attempted murder. No matter how I tried to convince myself though, it always seemed to fall back to the dream, and wondering what she had seen.

Her eyes were starting to scare me, the way she looked through me, or saw something that I didn't. Waking up from a shared dream was spooky enough, but having her poking around in a dream I didn't remember just scared the holy hell out of me. I was relieved when we got down to the stream, and the girls started setting up to spend the day there. In a few minutes I would be a mile up the trail, and out of range of her incredulous gaze. As I was getting ready to walk up the trail she stopped what she was doing and stared at me. "Be careful," she said.

"What is it, Sarah? What did you see?"

She tilted her head at me, thinking of the word, still looking through me. "*Nothing*," she said. "I saw *nothing*." She shrugged. "Just be careful up there."

Karen gave me a hug and patted my cheek. "Really Aaron, be careful."

I shook my head. It was all a trick, some creepy ghost story to freak me out and mindfuck me. "I'll be fine. I'll see you when we get back to L.A."

Geoff followed me up to the top of the rocks and kicked off his sandals. "You should follow the stream on the left bank for the first couple hundred feet. It's easier. After that you have to cross to the other side. The canyon splits a couple hundred feet from there. Just keep to the cliffs, and follow the dry riverbed. It'll lead you all the way up there."

"How far is it?"

"You'll be walking for a couple hours, at least." He pulled off his shirt and dropped his trunks. "And watch for snakes. They'll be hiding under rocks this time of day, and if you get an ankle near one, they'll bite it." He stretched his arms and back. I checked my shoelaces and tried to seem comfortable with the whole nudity thing. "A rattlesnake bite would probably knock you out or kill you before you got back to us, let alone down to the hospital."

"I've got a knife with me." I patted my satchel. "If I get bit I'll just cut around the bite and suck out the poison."

He chuckled. "How about you just watch your step."

I waved, set my shoulder strap and tilted the brim of my hat down over my eyes. "I'll be fine. I was a Boy Scout."

He chuckled again. "Crow every once in a while, just to let us know that you're still up there."

"You think you'll hear me?"

"Probably not, but who knows." He turned like he was going to jump and paused. "If you get scared and start running back, take it easy. The boulders are unstable sometimes. I'd feel awful if you twisted your ankle up there."

"If I'm not back by sunset, send the Swedish bikini team in after me."

"I don't even think Sarah would walk up there after you, so don't get yourself hurt." He made as if to give me a hug, but he was naked and all, and I couldn't do it. I grabbed his hand and shook it and gave him the rugged adventurer smirk. He just laughed. "Go get 'em, Cap'n."

I crowed. He crowed back and did a cannonball off the rock, splashing down into the pool below. Through the branches, I could see Karen and Sarah, already stripped down, mermaiden basking on the rocks at the edge of the pool.

The first mile of the trail wandered along beside the stream. Palm trees hung over pools, sunlight playing against the rain smoothed granite. Dragon flies and gnats skipped over the surface of the water. The refracted light danced against the boulders, rendering the whole scene in granite iridescence. It was entirely as Geoff had described it, the feeling that I might be the first human to walk there for centuries.

In spite of the secluded desert feel, there was most certainly a presence. Although most of the petroglyphs were further downstream, it seemed that the ancient tribes that had formerly inhabited the canyon left themselves everywhere in whispers. I expected to climb a set of boulders and come upon some ghostly collection of young women washing clothes, or more frightening yet, find a solitary man peering at me from behind a screen of palm fronds. Maybe the presence was exactly what Geoff and Sarah's mountaineering friend had felt, but it was benign to me, as harmless as the sense of antiquity one gets from old stone walls.

The snakes at least, were some sort of danger. Something to fear and watch for. Mostly I just hopped from boulder to boulder, and strolled along the dirt path that ran along the streams. The plants beside the pools draped shadows over the surface of the water. I squatted down and splashed it over my face. It was cool, and eased the sunburn a little. As the ripples calmed, Noskivvies appeared, blonde lock hanging over one eye. *You were expecting Grendel's mom, maybe?* He grinned back from the surface of the pool, sunbaked and slightly swollen faced from dehydration. *You didn't hike all the way up here to find a fucking monster, did you?* I hunted through my satchel for a cigarette, lit it, and knelt next to the pool. *You did! You hiked clear the fuck out here to find some sort of dragon to slay.* He laughed. *Man, you are a special sort of dumbass, aren'tcha. Shouldn't you be wearing a helmet for this sort of dashing excursion?*

"Fuck," I said.

He laughed and leaned back to smoke with me. *Well it's good to see you too, Desprecio.*

"They told me there was something dangerous up here."

Well speak for yourself, but some people consider me dangerous.

"Yeah, I'm sure you're the scourge of the sandbox, right?"

It just so happens that I'm a bloodthirsty pirate.

I started laughing. After a few good guffaws, I couldn't stop laughing. "Bloodthirsty pirate. Oh yeah, I'll bet."

I killed a god.

"You beat up a computer programmer with a foam bat."

I kissed his girlfriend, too.

"Oh yeah, now that's what I call bloodthirsty."

You think you got a better story to tell them?

"Oh not this 'them' thing again."

You still don't see them?

"Are there a few of them up there?"

Oh at least a couple dozen or so.

"Great." I stood up, glanced up the canyon further, and back towards the falls where Geoff and the girls were. "This is bullshit, man."

Don't look at me, man. I was perfectly happy hanging out at the bar.

"No. They told me there was a ghost up here."

What the fuck do you want? I can find a couple tadpoles or something. You can battle them with yer little ballpoint pen, show 'em who's boss.

I started back down the path. He hid under boulders, chasing me down. *Snakes, you want snakes? I got those. Venemous ones. Kill you in a few heartbeats, right?* I jumped from rock to rock, bouldering back down the canyon. It was easier than the walk up.

Where do you think you're going? He clung to a pond as I made my way through the reeds beside it.

"Home," I said.

She left yer ass. She doesn't want to have anything to do with us.

"What do you mean, 'us'?"

You know. You, me, them.

"Who are they?"

Fuck if I know, man, but they're starting to think yer a Sally.

Life amongst the winged

Sarah and I set up lounge chairs on the rock outcropping. To either side the drop was a decent one, and into stone, but the moon hung high and bright enough that the boulders were blue and looked every bit like we rested on a cloud bank. We clutched tall glasses of vodka and cranberry and stared up at the sky. We sipped our drinks and made small talk. Sarah adjusted her chair and reclined.

The night had a sound all its own, in the wind through the chaparral, our little friend Cream Cheese barking in the underbrush, crickets in the tall grass, that sort of thing. The longer we sat silent, the more sounds we heard, and I was close to dozing off before she spoke.

"I've always believed that I'm here for a reason." She glanced out over the valley.

"Me too," I said, from a place near the dreaming. Almost sleeping. "But I begin to wonder if we all have to believe that. Otherwise what's the point?"

She nodded. "But it's so real to me."

I opened my eyes to see the lights in the valley, and saw the place grow dark. The lights burned out and the desert turned black. Then, a flame at a time, small fires started up, lanterns were lit, torches lined the walkways, and the twinkling of cooking fires and burn barrels lit up the floor again, casting it in a dancing orange. The city itself seemed tiny, and circular, people living clustered together. Was that my vision, or hers? When I glanced at her, she had her eyes closed and faced the breeze. Again the city below was streetlamps, neon, and traffic lights, an electric lit puddle of bustling evening.

"I get the feeling like whatever it is we're here for, it's already happening," I said.

She glanced over and smiled comfortably. “Yeah, I think so too.” She sipped her drink. “But how can we be sure?”

I thought about it. It might be as much delusion as anything else. It is too easy to imagine monsters hiding in the shadows. “I don’t know.” I looked at her.

She turned to look back at me, her sleepy eyes patient, but waiting.

“Tell me where the place is,” I said, “and I’ll go plant your garden.”

Meditation engine

The first few minutes were awkward. Getting back on the bike, aiming for the onramp, getting it back up to speed. We were Rosinante and rider, not the brutal amalgam of flesh, fuel and steel. I dropped it into fourth, rolled on a few miles and got her warm again.

I hit the 101northbound. It was a longer ride, but I figured it might be easier than the straight-shot marathon drag race up the 5 freeway. We cut across the endless convoy of eighteen wheelers, tucked and settled up to speed. She breathed easier at ninety. The hum of the engine became the low throbbing bass line. My hands and feet buzzed. My body matched the frequency. I tried to harmonize, to match the note, but it made my teeth and jaw rattle. I sang, I talked to myself, I sang some more. Eventually the signposts outnumbered the thoughts, and the *nothing* saturated me. My heart beat clipped the dashed lines. My breath became negligible.

I was standing at a bus stop in Ellensburg, wondering if she'd show. I was riding back to the Tri-cities, without any sleep. We were laying in the grass by the river, playing chess. I was falling asleep with her head on my chest and the sun through the willow branches overhead. I woke up kissing in a raft, floating down the river, her body wrapped around mine. She smelled of sunblock and mosquito repellent. And holding her as the bus was getting ready to leave, I slipped my ring on her finger and it fit. "It's proof of something where *nothing* seems to exist." I told her, and we kissed goodbye. I passed out for an hour and woke up after sunset. I was cramped in a bus seat, between a fat hippy and the window. Outside, the pine trees clawed at the sky and it took me a while to realize that the stink was coming from me, the smell of sweat and sun and river water. My pant legs were muddy and my shoes were wet. I was all sun burnt.

After a few hours riding, whatever was, whatever would be, peeled gently away like an old skin, and there was only what is, forever and ever. Amen. This was the Zen they spoke of. A single mass of intertwined metal and flesh, the throbbing pulse of us together, striving forward. I wish that you were with me there, Habibi. When I was *nothing*, less than *nothing*, and we were merely the impression of movement into empty space.

Ka-chunk

Hit a pothole at ninety-five, caught a little air and landed hard. Lost the license plate and the gas cut out. Threw the choke open and idled five miles to the next exit. Found a public beach to park it and figured I was probably going to have to sell her and buy a train ticket. A couple hundred miles from Encinitas, and she quit. I thought about trying to pawn it off on the surfers loading up in the corner of the lot, but figured they wouldn't have that much cash on them. I cursed, I chainsmoked, I checked out the surf. Nice form with a short, clean right. On the plus side, if Mat hadn't fixed that bracket, that probably would've been the pothole that killed me. Took an hour of pacing and cussing before I resolved to make a phone call.

I started her up again and rode the open choke down into the city looking for a gas station or some tools. Found that I could shift gears alright and we picked up enough speed to match traffic. I remember Ventura, remember driving all over that fucking city looking for a bathroom when we first moved to California. Ventura's why Habibi hates Cali. Paved from one end to the other and *nothing* but shops. It's like one huge strip mall peppered with car lots.

I parked it at a mini mart. Bought a hot dog, a coke, a Butterfinger and a calling card. I powered down the hot dog and hovered around the payphone. There was no answer so I left some babbling message about how much I love her.

A guy pulled up in a big, flat-black station wagon, middle-aged at least, dark greasy hair and a goatee. Leaned on a cane and nodded at me as he hobbled into the mart. I tried to call my dad but he wasn't in the office. Last time I pulled a dumb stunt like this I called from the Buttonwillow truckstop. He didn't help at all. Told me which place had the best coffee, though.

I looked over the bike, worked on the Butterfinger some. A guy with a cane came out smiling. "What kind of bike?"

"Kawasaki."

"I used to ride." He nodded, looked down at his leg. "Can't anymore."

"Sorry." Now I'm expecting some sort of lecture on how dangerous they are, how he fucked up his leg sliding off a Harley or whatever. "They say there are two kinds of people on motorcycles…"

"Oh I didn't fuck it up getting in a wreck." He glanced over the bike. "Hundred and first." He shrugged. "Shrapnel. Took it in the back and legs."

"Shit."

"My own damn fault. Anyone who'd jump out of a perfectly good airplane is either stupid or crazy. Guess I was both." He climbed into his car. "How far ya headed?"

"Eastern Washington."

"Long hauler."

"Gotta get back to my girl."

"Stupid or crazy, man." He nodded. "Have a nice ride."

He pulled out. I tried to call home again, but she didn't answer. I guess maybe that was enough, though. Hopped on Rosi to choke her to a gas station. Idled along in the bike lane, eating my candy bar. She perked right up after a block. Polished off the Butterfinger and pulled my helmet on as I slid back into traffic. Eased her onto the freeway and drove the same five miles a couple times looking for my missing license plate. Found it and a horseshoe as well. Looked like the plate hit the tire on the landing, busted the bracket off. Funny, but I think I remember Mat telling me that would happen. I unbent the plate and strapped it to my bag with a bungee. Figured on bolting the horseshoe to the front as soon as I found some tools.

My hands were sunburnt up to the wrists

I waited out the sun in an outlet mall parking lot near Paso Robles. The security guard eyed me. Rosinante ticked as she cooled off. I was two-hundred-some odd miles from San Francisco and getting further from the girl. She wasn't taking my calls. Rosi was apparently pissed off as well. It was the second time in two-hundred miles that her engine cut out at ninety. She was doing it and then she wasn't, and I idled the few miles to the next exit. Once again Southern California pounded me under its freakish gravity.

I got the feeling like Rosi had a thing for that girl. Every time I got to worrying about Habibi, Rosi crapped out. She was running on faith. If I didn't have it, she wasn't going to make it. I tried to start her again. No go. I placed a couple collect calls, nobody answered. Well, Pop answered and promised to call the girl and leave her the number of the payphone. She was probably out, and there was no guarantee she'd call. Like I said, she wasn't talking to me.

Maybe Rosi quit so I would take a few minutes. Maybe she quit so I'd avoid an accident or have to call Habibi collect from the side of the road. Same thing. Guess it wasn't too bad. At least she would get a few messages. She couldn't say I didn't try.

Meanwhile, the mini-mall speakers piped in this sappy soft'n'easy superhits of the sixties and seventies. Just what I needed. Lovesongs. Did I mention my theory on hell? Minimalls and easy listening.

While I was in the gas station buying a microwave Philly Cheesesteak and a 24ouncer, there was this song playing. Country Western. Paint me a Birmingham. Damnitall.

We were at her sister's graduation in Virginia. She was fooling around with the dials on the radio. Said there was no good music on the radio in Eastern Washington, so she was getting into country. I figured she was joking, but I couldn't tell. She was full of surprises. She went on about how they told a story. This song came on the radio and she started singing it. None of us knew what a Birmingham was. Maybe Alabama, maybe a style of house, maybe an artist, but she sang on and on about how it should have a wraparound porch and a girl out there waiting. Put her in a cotton dress, make it early spring. It sounded pretty. The girl, the house, but all I saw was Habibi on the porch in Eastern Washington, jeans and a t-shirt, a bandana tying her hair back. I doubted she'd be there come midsummer.

The full moon rose, golden to the southeast. Sun went down and I hoped Rosi had cooled off. Pop guessed the bike was vaporlocked. I guessed she was lovelorn. Maybe that was just me. Yeah vaporlocked. I needed to start thinking rationally, quit this deranged romanticist superstition. Motorcycles don't know shit about symbols.

The clock on the tank said it was almost nine but it was wrong. It stopped a few times on the ride. I'd like to think it was light speed, but I got to thinking that if that were the case, all the other clocks would be slow and Rosi'd be a couple hours ahead. I was actually moving in reverse. Too quickly.

There was still no answer, and Rosinante wouldn't roll on the throttle. Habibi wouldn't give me a chance to explain and Rosi wouldn't accept radio silence. I was fucked. Pragmatic motorcycle mechanics my ass. Either way, I was still fucked. I figured there wasn't much point in sitting around.

She idled on her open choke. Twenty five in first, thirty five in second. I teased her throttle up to about forty.

Oh you gotta be joking. Thirty-seven miles per hour?

"I should have known you'd show up once it got dark."

In the darkness, we make monsters, simply to pretend that we are not alone.

"Yeah, well, I've got enough monsters."

Fuck else you got to do?

"I have to go home."

Dead men have no home.

"I'm not dead yet."

Funny, this place feels like a tomb.

I glanced around at the scenery, rolling green hills and wide open spaces cast in pale blue moonlight. "Sure, I can see how you'd say that. Nothing like a stretch of perfect pristine freeway to make you feel claustrophobic."

Or delusional.

"You are my delusion."

Just me? And how can you be sure of that?

"I'm talking to myself."

And your self is trying to tell you that you're imagining the whole thing. Interesting paradox, yes?

"How can I be dead if I'm driving back to Habibi?"

Sometimes dead men take decades to crawl into their graves.

"Do you have to be so dark?"

It's a rough life for a shadow, constantly tied to the heels of some ambling half-wit monkey.

"How about you ease up for a few hours."

You poor bastard, maybe you should take it easy. Slow down a little. He laughed. *Does this thing have a reverse?*

"We're not going back there."

Back where?

"Back to SoCal."

And exactly where do you think we're going?

"Home."

A hole fulla fear.

"I have no fear anymore. I'm chasing love and light. I'm going to get the girl."

Fear forces us to light a candle, to push back the dark, to cast another shadow against the wall. Like lighting another candle is making another friend. Some dim lit body, bustling in the periphery, like a body in the mirror behind a dark bar. At least it's some sort of company.

"I only wish I was sitting in a bar right now."

Oh, I wouldn't go back there for a while. You made a total ass of yourself last night.

"Last night I was sleeping on Geoff and Karen's floor."

Last night you drank your last forty bucks in whiskey and beers, sang the Dead Kennedy's "Too drunk to fuck" *at the karaoke machine, and picked a fight with some old guy with a hearing aid who kept calling you the young Faulkner.*

"Faulkner's a boob."

Yeah, yeah, heard that about ten times last night.

"Where do you get this shit from?"

Then you called your precious Habibi from a payphone, threatened to walk the twelve miles across town to her house, and ended up replacing all the clock faces in the house with old porn you found under the bathroom sink. He laughed. *Lue's a little pissed about that. Nice touch, by the way, telling them that I did it while you were passed out. Must be convenient to blame all your dumbest stunts on some internalized imaginary enemy.*

I tried to ignore him, focus on the road ahead, focus on the pops and sputters coming from the engine, hoping each one would kick out the vaporlock and get me rolling again.

Of course, it's insane to make friends with the shadows, but sometimes you have no other choice. It's either that, or just keep pretending that they're monsters. My question is, if we are all alone here, then what do we have to fear?

"What's with this 'we' shit again?"

Hey man, it's your happy little hell hole, don't go calling me out on plurality.

"What am I doing?"

Just keep driving.

"Nobody is supposed to believe in this sort of shit." I tried downshifting again, to see if I could blow it out, but she just sputtered on the throttle. "We're supposed to read about it, watch it on TV or in a movie. We're supposed to fantasize about it when we're working, but we're sure as hell not supposed to do it."

Fantasize about it. I like that. You are a special sort of dumbass, aint'cha? Hey, can I ask you something? What makes this shit so real to you?

"This is truly living." I relaxed a little over the tank, let a little off the muscles in my shoulders, and felt them crumple. I nodded, smiled, and glanced over at the traffic rushing past me. "This is life on the edge. Everybody dies, but not everybody truly lives."

You get that shit off a fortune cookie, or what?

"Seriously, man, we're lucky to be here."

Yeah, yeah. Carpe Diem and all that crap.

"No, I mean, this is freedom, right here. This is exactly what they're talking about." I flicked open my visor and grinned out at the headlight running the margin of the highway. "We can get on a rusted out piece of shit motorcycle, and bust ass across the states if we want to. We can scrape dimes to run the coast, or hop a train to New York if we have to. This is freedom. The great

American roadtrip. This is what it's all about. And on a fucking motorcycle? Hell yeah, Hallelujah."

Yeah, and I'm sure that creeping up the edge of the freeway at thirty-eight miles per hour might seem romantic and all, but I really fail to see the point here.

"The point is that we can."

Do you smell something?

"I smell Freedom."

Nah, man, it smells like old socks or something.

"A little optimism, huh?"

At least they're probably ours.

"Is there some sort of medication that I can get on that might fix you?"

Well the drugs we're on aren't helping much.

Safehouse

Last year, Habibi and I spent Thanksgiving with her old family friend in Paso Robles. A woman named Dorothy. Wine and art aficionado. She drinks and talks. Nice lady. I figured if I could make it there I could find a phone, e-mail, maybe a place to sleep. I rode the shoulder for ten miles before I passed the first Paso Robles exit. Got off 101 and found an intersection that I recognized. Just as I hit the stoplight, Rosi's throttle kicked in again. She may know shit about symbols, but she's got a way with forcing safety stops. Thought about riding on but then I got to figuring the reststop was a good idea. I could get a message to Habibi. Let her know that I'm still going. She's been worried. That's why she's angry. The fear is fucking with her.

It was pretty late when I pulled up at Dorothy's. I didn't want to knock, but the door was open, TV on, and the dogs were already barking when I got to the gate. Dorothy came out in her nightgown, cussing, and found me there, probably looking a little ominous. I put my hands up while one of the dogs growled and gnawed at my jeans. "I'm Emira's boyfriend, I was here for thanksgiving."

"Oh, Aaron." She nodded. "What are you doing?"

"Motorcycle's breaking down."

"Well come on in." She kept swatting at the big black dog. "He's blind. He doesn't like men. What do you need? A phone? A place to stay? Come on in. Bed's there, it's made. Phone's in there. I was just falling asleep." She picked up a wine glass from the coffee table and set it in the kitchen. "You want a glass of wine?" But she was already pouring it. The dog kept chewing on my sneakers. "Give Mackers a treat so he knows you're friendly. I'm going to bed." She wandered down the hall. "And finish the rest of that bottle. It'll be bad by tomorrow."

"Thanks, Dorothy." A peculiar hostess, but I was awful glad to find her. I fed both the dogs treats and tried to call Habibi. The line was busy. Called Blake and told him that I wasn't going to make it tonight. He was sad. Said he had three guitars, a few harmonicas and some friends over, but he had tomorrow off, so it'd work out. Tried to call the girl again, but the line was still busy. I hoped she wasn't trying to call that payphone. Hoped she wasn't too worried. I told her I'd get there. Mackers started chewing at my shoe again, so I gave him another treat.

I woke up all wrong, disoriented, straight from the seeming death of a dreamless sleep only to find myself in a big soft bed, a big black dog staring at me from the edge of the mattress. When I moved, the dog growled. Mackers was my sleep, personified, dark and somewhat ominous, his eyes cloudy and grey. Kitchen sounds clattered down the hall, and a TV news reporter talked about the continuing war in Iraq, escalating violence in Bagdad. The deadliest day in Afghanistan. I rubbed my face and the dog growled again. When I sat up to look around, he barked. "Mackers!" she hollered from the kitchen. The dog peered over his shoulder. Dorothy appeared in the doorway. "Sorry about that Aaron. We don't get many visitors." She came in to grab Mackers' collar and drag him out. "Go back to sleep."

I cracked my neck and stretched. After a night in a real bed, my shoulders had petrified somehow. "Nah, it's okay. I should get back on the road."

"What's your hurry? Take your time." She pushed and kicked at Mackers to get him out of the room. He might've outweighed her by a few pounds of fur. "Take a shower. The towels are fresh. There's soap in there, use it. Do you drink coffee? I'll make you some. How do you take it? Nevermind, just take it easy, there's plenty of time." She pointed me towards the adjoining bathroom.

After she closed the door, I got up and made my way into the shower. It had all the frilly accoutrements, the pink bathroom rugs with matching towels, bowls of potpourri on the back of the toilet, a variety of shampoos, conditioners, soaps, and bodywashes. After the rustic cold water washes at the cabin, it was like wandering into a five star spa. By the time I got out, the mirrors were all fogged, and wiping them clean, I found that my flesh was all pink. I pulled on my road stinking clothes and made my way out to a kitchen that smelled of Bacon and fresh baked biscuits. The table was set for one, bowls, plates and pans steaming at the center. Dorothy poured me a big mug of coffee and set it next to the plate. "You take cream and sugar? No? well there you go. Eat something." She patted the single table setting, and slid back into the kitchen to wash up the dishes.

It was an awful lot of food for one uninvited houseguest. I would have told her that I don't eat breakfast, generally, but it was all there, eggs, bacon, potatoes, fresh biscuits. I took my place and sipped the coffee. It was the best coffee I'd had in weeks at least. Better for the surprise. I would have taken the coffee alone and saved her the trouble of cooking a breakfast, but to refuse her hospitality would have been a great sin.

"So what are you doing all the way out here, and why are you on that ridiculous motorcycle?"

I served myself eggs, and picked a few slices of bacon off the platter. "I'm driving to Eastern Washington, driving back to Emira."

She glanced over. "I heard that she was up there, that she left you again."

I nodded.

"Her mother is worried about her."

I nodded again.

"So you're driving up there, on that?" She motioned towards Rosinante. "That seems a little, well, you know, I just don't see the point."

I shrugged. "Love makes us do crazy things, right?"

"But for her? I mean, god bless her little heart, god bless the whole damn family, but doesn't that seem a little crazy?"

"Maybe." I nodded and took a bite.

"You know, I've known that family for years, and, well, after their father left, well, it caused a lot of problems with the family. And the way he left, well, it's no wonder they have problems with men."

I nodded.

"And then to move in with that man, well, you know, it's just a shame."

I nodded again.

"And now, to see what they're still going through. I mean Emira, that poor girl. How could she ever be with a man, always wondering if he would do the same thing." She dried her hands on a towel and brought her teacup out to the table, taking a seat next to me. "I mean it's no wonder that you two have problems with your relationship."

"Yeah, she should have come with a warning label."

"I thought she did." She sipped her tea. "She has such sad eyes."

I nodded again, and looked down at my breakfast. The last of the eggs, the potatoes, the half eaten slices of bacon. The table was laden for a feast, but I ate alone. Mackers started chewing on my shoe again.

"Mackers, knock it off!" she swatted the dog with a rolled up napkin.

"I can't thank you enough, Dorothy."

She smiled. "We don't get many guests," she said.

After the breakfast dishes were cleared, Dorothy excused me to smoke a cigarette. I stood on the back patio next to the murky swimming pool. Most of the backyard was overgrown, except for a few immaculate garden plots set off to one side. The pool was still covered, and a thick patina of fallen leaves speckled the surface.

"Nasty habit." Dorothy said, coffee pot in hand.

"I have worse."

She shook her head. She may not be my mom, but she was somebody's mom, and she gave me one of those mom looks that just made me feel guilty about the whole thing.

"Say, as long as you're here, you mind helping me with something? Jaime has this old boat back here, but I need to move it out of the way. I've been thinking about terracing this hill over here, and planting a flower garden…"

It was nearly noon by the time I got back to repacking my gear. Dorothy was already on the phone with Rose, Emira's mom. I bungeed my bag down, making sure that the license plate was mostly visible, even if the tags were expired.

Dorothy paced the front porch, watching me pack, all the while assuring Rose that I was doing well. As I pushed Rosinante out of the sideyard, Dorothy told the phone to hold on a second.

"Thanks, Dorothy."

She nodded. "You be careful out there, Aaron."

"I will."

"Now I mean it. Don't go getting yourself killed over a girl, you hear me?"

The last of the lost boys

A few blocks from Blake's house in Berkeley there were whole food stores and co-ops, organic produce, hemp products, cultural sensitivity, love for all mankind, and all the rest of that crap.

On Blake's block there were liquor stores, low riders, and pig iron barbeque restaurants. The streets were lined with litter. The lawns were turning brown in the early summer sun. Clusters of men stood around cars, stripped down to their T-shirts, listening to music, watching the women walk past. This was the Berkeley that Oakland never surrendered, and there is an easy comfort in knowing that I could walk into any store on the block, buy a single shot banger of bourbon and a 40 oz. bottle of malt liquor for just a few bucks.

Blake's house was in the middle of the block. I pulled Rosinante up to the curb, flipped off the key and kicked down the stand. Across the street half a dozen guys stood around a lowered Lexus, smoking a blunt and watching me shed my gear. "Hey." One of the guys walked halfway across the street, looking over the bike. "What is that thing?"

"It used to be a Kawasaki," I said.

He nodded. "You been ridin' it hard." He took a pull from his blunt.

"No other way," I said.

"It's smokin'." He pointed at the pipe.

"More than I do these days."

He laughed.

"You mind if I get a pull off that?" I eyed his blunt.

He looked a little surprised and glanced back at the rest of the guys watching us. "This ain't no cigar."

"I hope not." I smiled.

"Yeah, a'ight." He handed me the blunt. I took a long drag and tried to pass it back.

He waved it off. "Hit it again."

I shrugged, exhaled and took another pull. "That's some decent shit."

He nodded. "Damn right." He smiled. "Cannabis club; cause I'm sick." He winked. "You know these guys here?" He pointed at Blake's house. The place looked a little rundown, paint peeling, a cushionless couch on the lawn, the bottom half of a mannequin jutting out of the bushes and a graveyard of bicycle parts scattered around the front porch.

"I know one of them at least."

He nodded. "These fuckers smoke some tasty chron."

"Yeah?"

"Yeah. Skinny fucker upstairs grows it."

"No shit?"

He nodded.

One of the guys from across the street hollered. He was big and tall with a shaved head. "Hey nigga, bring that shit back here."

"Shut the fuck up." He waved the guy off.

"Hey," the guy across the street hollered again. "Hey, that thing gonna blow up or what?" A couple of the guys chuckled.

"Not yet," I said.

"We ride it?" the guy called.

The guy with the blunt turned toward them. "Nigga, you can't ride a mothafuckin' bicycle."

The rest of the guys laughed.

"I'm gonna go see if they're in there."

"They in there." He nodded. "You see that boy Mike, you tell him my glaucoma's gettin' bad."

I laughed. "Yeah, mine too."

He took a drag, nodded me off, and strolled back across the street to murmurs and laughter.

Blake's got a soul like the whole Salvation Army band crammed into a mixed tape for a girl. He's the sort of guy that's good at taking something mundane, wiping away the dust, and handwriting a label for it. His bedroom was in the back of the house, a mattress on the floor, covered in a Care Bear quilt and a huge pile of the stuffed pastel bears, all neatly arranged. He had a simple wood writing desk facing the back window. It was covered with stacks of papers, spiral notebooks, and a few photo albums. Two more walls were entirely shelves lined with row upon row of books, albums, and video cassettes. A few dozen Pez dispensers lined the edges of the shelves like a cartoon armory. A mismatched stereo was on a low shelf, stacking up to a turntable. In the far corner beside the other window, there was a wooden chair, an eight track recorder, a few guitars, a microphone and headphones. He stood in the middle of the room, scratching the back of his head. Despite the fact that he seemed to live in squalor, in a shitty ass neighborhood, his room was an immaculately clean pastel plastic wonderland. "Have I shown you my new tattoo?" He pulled up a pant leg to reveal the fresh black silhouette of Quixote, Sancho, and a few windmills in the distance. "I went to Spain this summer." He reached up to a line of black binders, pulled a volume of photographs from a shelf. "I took over a hundred rolls of film."

Blake was always in or out of Love. Either way he never went about it half-assed. What started in glimmering mixed tapes and poetry ended in ink, cigarette burns, and dog eared scrawl on random scraps of paper. The nice thing is that he documented it all, so it was that much easier to catch up on a visit.

He went to Spain with a girl, but since then it ended. She was something precious to him, but it was apparently getting easier to let her go. He met another girl not too long ago, and she turned the tide of Blake's afflicted blood. A few minutes later I was on the floor, reclining against a pile of plush bears, a stack of black binders beside me, a bottle of beer in one hand, and Blake offering me a packed bong. At long last I had found some semblance of civilization.

As the sun dropped in the sky, the bodies gathered at the door. Roger came from teaching guitar to a fifteen-year-old, picked up an acoustic, and sat strumming on the bed. Gabriel finished up at the coffee shop, dropped a six pack of IPA on the floor, and pulled up a chair. Justin got off work at the print shop, and despite the fact that he didn't drink or smoke anymore, he arrived with beer, a bottle of liquor, and his bass guitar. By the time the night was spread out proper across the sky, the available band of brothers strummed and picked easily from their seats around the empty floor.

I wasn't the only one who'd been away for a while. It seemed like the rest of the boys had grown apart as well. Maybe they lived a few miles away from each other, but their lives were all changing. Roger had a new girlfriend, Gabriel had broken up with his. Justin, despite the fact that he was still single, was back to drinking a lot of pineapple juice, because he heard somewhere that it was supposed to make his cum taste better. Now he was looking for someone to help him verify it.

Blake passed his photos around, narrating the pages of snapshots while Roger plucked old jazz tunes out of the acoustic. At some point, Justin picked up his bass, and for all the years and miles that had grown between us, we played our parts like we'd been practicing, waiting for the night when the brothers would gather again, maybe for the last time. Maybe at some point, we were a movement, a handful of particles orbiting a point of light, but we had lost our nucleus, and with it, all of our potential energy. He wasn't with us anymore, but nobody wanted to admit it. Things had changed. We didn't talk about him, though. We talked about our jobs, our girlfriends and exes, our triumphs and tragedies, and told stories like we were hammering petroglyphs into the walls of our own personal ruts.

I wanted to show them a picture, to prove her real. I wanted to pull a snapshot from my pocket and tell them: "This is her. This is my Habibi." But all I had in my wallet was a sonogram of her heart with some doctor's fading Magic Marker scribbles at the edges. She had mitrovalve prolapse. It was kind of like her heart worked so hard that sometimes it skipped a beat. Because she had a picture of it, it was a genetic defect. Funny, but I always felt like when she was close, her condition was sort of contagious.

As the night wore on and the beers got low, I showed them the shot anyway.

The photo of her afflicted heart.

A case of the 24 hour glaucoma

Blake sat up and threw his feet over the side of the bed. He rubbed his face and blinked at me. “Fuck.” He got up and staggered out into the bathroom. His bedroom looked like a Care Bear stare had hit a disco ball. Cheery eyed furry pastel soldiers lay strewn about the room in various drunken party poses, clutching 24 oz cans of Olde English and empty forty bottles, passed out in armchairs, sprawled over drunken scrawl-filled pages on the desk. Some looked over open binders of Blake’s photographs, others clung to the bookshelves, sprawled in fields of toppled pez dispensers.

Blake wandered back into the room, glanced around. “Fuck,” he said again, and chuckled. “Who wants to smoke some pot?” he asked the entire room, as if somewhere in the corner, a squadron of stuffed bears might march the bong over like an artillery cannon.

“What the hell.” I sat up and kicked the rest of the sleeping bag off.

I followed Blake a few blocks to the corner liquor store. He wandered in, walked back to the beer fridge, and pulled out two 24 oz cans of OE. At the counter, he asked for two bangers of whiskey and two packs of cigarettes. He got two small paper bags and walked back out to the curb with five bucks in his hand. “For coffee,” he said.

“Ah shit, man, you don’t have to do that,” I said.

He pushed it at me. I’d like to insist on my no, but the fact was, that five spot looked like a baseball sized lump of gold in his hand. Two gallons at least. He distributed drinks and smokes. We paper bagged our beers, downed the bangers, and packed our cigarettes.

"I'm glad you're here, man." He offered his beer for salute.

"Glad to be here."

He checked the time on his cell phone and pushed it back into his pocket. "I'm off work around six, and then I have band practice."

I zigzagged lazily down the residential streets, nursing my can. Not even noon yet and I was already sporting a decent smirk and a nice buzz besides. I checked out random furniture with free signs, and dug through a few boxes of sundry items. I picked out a few books that caught my eye, and stopped myself from carrying home an old kid's carseat, figuring that there wasn't much backseat left on Rosinante. After a few blocks the gardens got less manicured. Weeds and grass grew tall and then dry and then the edge of the sidewalks weren't curbside gardens anymore, but worn out dirt walkways, or lanes of asphalt beside the concrete. Grass sprouted between the cracks and everywhere the asphalt crumbled, the green grew up. By the time I got to the street with the liquor stores and cops, I realized that I was back in my neighborhood again. I finished my can, left it on a mailbox, and walked into the first market I saw. A five spot covered a forty of HG800, a banger of beam, and a candy bar. So much for coffee. Or gasoline.

I found my way back to the house and got inside alright, but I sat down on the front steps and cracked the forty and lit another cigarette. Already the sidewalk was heating up, and a new shopping cart rested against a lamppost a few feet from Rosinante. I flipped through the books I picked up.

I was only out there a few minutes when Mike came out in his pajama bottoms and a holey T-shirt. I glanced over my shoulder and nodded. He had a cigarette in hand and dusted the ash off the railing before he leaned against it. "What are you up to?" He squinted through the smoke.

I raised my beer.

He nodded and snorted, smiling wide and stoney-eyed. "That your bike?"

I nodded.

He walked to the edge of the top step and looked it over. "What year is that?"

"Eighty seven, I think."

"Looks like a piece of shit." He blew smoke at it.

I nodded. "It is."

He laughed. "Where you going?" he asked.

To hell if I don't change my ways, "Eastern Washington."

"Fuck," he said.

"Yeah."

"You really think that thing is going to make it?"

"If the terrorists don't get me first."

"Terrorists, dude?" He gave a stoney gutteral laugh, sputtering pot smoke at me. "Fuckers across the street aren't gonna get killed by Osama Bin Laden. It's gonna be a guy from a few blocks away that's got something to prove. Blake's gonna get killed by some guy that comes in to hold up the grocery store. You'll probably get killed by some gun-toting redneck that thinks you're a faggot or a terrorist." He blurted a loud cough of a laugh and took another puff off the joint.

"What about you?" I asked.

He shook his head. "I ain't gonna die." He smiled. "Because all I do is smoke too much damn pot and hide in my house all day." He passed me the joint.

"So that's the only way to live, huh? Get high and hide from everybody?"

"It's the American way, dude." He nodded.

I woke up on the couch, my jacket for a blanket, and the bitter taste of bad beer fermenting in the back of my throat. It was already evening, and Blake's roommate just walked in the front door. He leaned his bike against the busted one in the front walkway. His pedal clips sounded like tap shoes down the hall. I sat up and rubbed my face, trying to work the blood back into a foggy brainbox. The evening was already setting in, the pale sky turning cobalt and indistinct clouds out the front window. I was thirsty, and felt the few days' rest wearing at my shoulders. As nice as it is to get back to my roots, I guess it's like the man said. I just wanted to get back to Habibi's arms; to feel her body pressed against mine for even so long as an evening. Maybe it was just another heartbeat, but it was hers, and when we were close, out of sympathy, I guess it was mine.

So hard that it had to skip a beat.

There was no way out yet, and I had maybe a gallon of gas worth of change in my pockets if I was lucky. William came into the living room with a joint, a lighter, and two beers. He cracked the caps and handed me the extra.

"How was work?" I asked.

He shrugged and paused before he lit the joint. "I got cut off by a guy in a BMW that almost put me into a mailbox." He blew at the ember and inspected his handiwork.

"That sucks," I said.

He shrugged. "I was going to put my lock through his back window, but I had to take a right to make my package."

I nodded like I knew what that meant, took another sip, and inspected the label again.

"So what's up with your bike?"

"*Nothing*," I said.

"I figured you broke down or something." He passed the joint and took a sip of his beer. "Blake said that you were just passing through."

I nodded. "Got no gas money." I took two quick puffs and passed it back.

"That sucks," he said. He took a puff, inspected the joint, and spitting lightly on his finger, he manicured the burn and took another long puff. "What are you going to do?" he asked, holding it in, but letting loose a lazy tendril. He passed the joint back.

I shrugged. "The way writes itself," I said. "Sometimes I just gotta wait."

He nodded, folding his hands as if in prayer and blew the rest into his clasped palms. "I hear ya."

I took a couple quick puffs, but it wasn't quick enough. Between the beer and the joint, I got the feeling like I wasn't going anywhere soon. I took another long gulp, hoping to speed up the process.

"Where you headed?" he asked.

I handed him the joint. "Home," I said. It was easier than explaining. I guess I waste a lot of time explaining lately.

He took the joint and puffed at it. "Where's home?" he asked. But it was already too late.

I leaned back on the couch, clutched my beer to my chest, and stared off through the window at the last lingering light. "HOME." I said, with everything I had left.

Know time

In the morning, Blake sat down next to me on the couch. I still had the beer bottle clutched in my hand, last few sips gone warm. Blake packed the bong and handed it to me. "It was good to see you again," he said.

I set my beer on the floor and took the bong. "What did I do?"

He shrugged. "I miss him."

I took a hit and nodded.

"When you're around, it's like he isn't dead."

I let the smoke slip out, wandering off to hang about the room. "Same here, man."

"They tell me that I sing about him too much." He took the bong.

"Who the fuck are they?"

"You know. Them."

"I keep hearing about them, but I still don't see them."

He nodded, smiled, and hit the bong.

"Fuck 'em if they can't take a joke, right?" He blew another ghost to life.

"Yeah."

He dug into his pocket and pulled out a wad of cash. "It's all I've got right now, but I figured it might help you get to Portland."

"You don't have to do that."

He shrugged. "I know."

"I probably can't pay you back anytime soon."

He nodded. "I know." He passed me the bong. "Sometime, when I'm passing through, you can return the favor."

I nodded, but we both knew he wouldn't be passing through any time soon.

"Is she worth it?"

I lit the bong and inhaled with a shrug. "Worth a shot at least." I let the smoke slip again.

He nodded. "Know time," he said.

I nodded back.

"Take care of yourself."

I smiled. "Not my choice anymore."

"It was good to see you."

We hugged hard, and then he left.

While I was tying on my sneakers, William took the chair across from me at the dining room table. He was dressed in his biking gear, and ready for work. He laid out a bunch of shake and started rolling joints. "So you think you'll make it?"

I smiled and snorted a laugh. "No choice now."

"There's always a choice." He finished twisting one up and licked the edge.

I leaned back in my chair. "Yes," I said. "I do fear that I will live through this one."

"Fear?"

I watched him start to roll another.

"It would be more romantic if I died along the way."

He looked up from his work and raised an eyebrow at me.

"I mean, as far as tragedies go, it's better if the hero dies."

"Better for who?" He licked the end of the second joint.

"I can't make it. They tell me there are no happy endings."

He screwed up his face and bent back over his work.

"I mean, happy endings are for fiction."

He licked the end of the third joint, compared it to the other two, and chose the thinnest of the three. "You read too much."

I was indignant. "I read the classics."

He took a long pull off the joint and inspected his work. "Yeah, well, I don't know much about books, but in real life we don't die like that." He passed off the joint.

I took it and inspected his handiwork. "Fair enough." I took a long pull.

"I mean, you have to give it a fair shot, at the very least."

"A fair shot?"

He took a pull. "Yeah, I mean, what happens if you live?"

"I don't know."

He handed back the joint. "Well that's real life."

I was already too stoned to deal with such preposterous concepts. I scowled, took a hit, and tried to hand him back the joint.

"Finish it," he said.

I glanced at the joint.

"And take these." He handed me the other two joints. "Safe journey."

"I can't," I said.

"Yeah, I know. That's your problem." He saluted me and walked down the hall. Lifting his bike from the others, he opened the door and set the front tire out the door. "You know that thing is leaking oil pretty bad?"

"Yeah."

"Alright, man, see you around." But I figured we both knew he wouldn't.

"Thanks, William."

He nodded, smiled, and walked away. Pedal clips like tap shoes all the way down the steps.

I packed the joints into my cigarette box, checked my gear, and made my way out to the bike. Strapping my gear down, I rediscovered that horseshoe I found on the 101. I pulled it out from under the straps and brought it in to Blake's desk. It still had a little horseshit on it, but I figured he wouldn't mind much.

I didn't have much else to give him.

Mach yes

Carving a track through Berkeley, and down into Oakland, Rosinante was pure street fighter. The late morning commuters stuck their lanes like autopilot automatons, jamming up behind any and every delay, waiting for someone to parallel park, or make a left turn at a signal. They banged against their steering wheels and swung their heads around, waiting for a chance to cut into the next lane. They cussed at each other, honked their horns, and yelled out the windows because someone cut them off or hit the brakes for a yellow light that they might have made.

There is a sense of freedom about a motorcycle which is impossible to describe to anyone who has never ridden one; the intoxicating impression of lightness. With the engine running up to the power band, it sounds like an old reciprocating engine airplane, the steady drone and the buffeting winds of uncaged momentum. I was infused with the sense of immortality and buoyancy that one feels astride a potentially deadly piece of machinery.

We moved like mercury through the clogged arteries of the concrete cityscape, a heavy metal liquid propelled by gravity and fate, propelled by manifest destiny and prophecy. We were not just invisible, but we had lost our solid state entirely and had become something liquid, gaseous, and then plasmatic. We became a matter beyond matter itself, composed of a material which had become inconceivable to science, a sense of something greater, like an idea, an impression, or a presence. Making our way through the city we were felt more than seen, and by the time that we passed, we were merely the lingering idea of the thing itself.

From Blake's house to the 205 freeway, for reasons which they might never be able to explain, the people began to feel restless, and trapped, and wished for something beyond the known walls of their personal ruts. They longed for freedom, true freedom, not just the ability to vote for their favorite American

Idol contestant, or choose which soda they liked best, or decide which color to paint the walls of their happy little domestic box trap, but the people began to feel, even for a brief moment, what it might be like to haul ass down a side street on a rusted out crotch rocket, hell-bent on their own personal quest for Habibi. Even for the split second space in time which is the drag strip distance between two traffic lights, they felt it, and they wanted more of it.

Blake filled my gas tank with his righteous, hard-earned dollar bills, and although it seemed like *nothing*, it was enough to inspire me. If Blake believed I could make it, enough to give me the last of his cash, then I had to believe.

We didn't materialize again until we were a few gallons gone, so much particulate matter collecting over the concrete a hundred miles away, the Yoshi pipe screaming hellfire and hauling down a sonic thunderclap behind us. Flesh, fuel, and steel.

Faster Rosinante. Lightspeed.

Hit and run

I was stuck again. Around noon. San Joaquin Valley. Rosi got hot, idled off the 5 onto the 99. We rolled off to the shoulder. I was pushing her too hard. I tried to sweet talk her some but it's not much help. I don't know if it was the radiator or the oil or whatever, I just don't think Rosi was designed for the long hauls. Too damn hot for it.

We crept down 99 at twenty-five for a few miles. Chapparal and sand gave way to three clusters of brand new tract homes. It looked like someone planned a city there, but it was still a ghost town. Miles of beige boxes lining empty streets, like huge stucco headstones.

The first sign of civilization was a 7/11. I asked the woman behind the counter for directions to a café. She pointed me toward a Starbucks. Rest stop-sized city and that was my big option. I pushed the bike into some shade and smoked a cigarette. Tires screeched, some guy yelled, a mint-green Jetta hauled ass around the corner and was gone. "Yer dead!" the guy screamed, chasing. People came out of shops, traffic slowed. "She knocked him into the ditch and drove off!" The people collected, murmuring. Further down there was a guy laying on the side of the road, clutching his knee. People crowded around him. I jumped on Rosinante, flipped the key, and hit the start button. She popped into first and died again. If Rosinante weren't vaporlocked I might have chased the Jetta down, but it wasn't going to happen at twenty-five miles per hour. My chance to be some sort of hero was blown on a burnt-out engine. Cars were stacked up pretty deep in the lane where the guy sat in the ditch. I didn't hear any sirens, and somebody said that he was fine; he'd be up in a few minutes. There was a lady selling shaved ice from a stand in front of the thrift shop next door. I asked her for a cafe, she asked somebody else. He pointed me in the opposite direction of Starbucks. Good enough.

A few chuggy miles at twenty and we rolled into neighborhoods with big green trees lining the streets. Someone must've irrigated the hell out of that city, as green as it was. Miles of desert wasteland surrounded a Better Homes and Gardens oasis. I hung a right onto Main Street looking for anything other than houses and idled into a shopping center. A few restaurants, a grocery store, nail salon, and a library. It was basically another minimall. The library was a nice touch. Guess if I had to wait a while I might as well spend a couple hours reading. The outer edge of the parking lot was lined with trees and apartments. I rolled up under a pine and tucked her into the shade. She ticked and cussed a little. The bank sign said it was ninety-four degrees and a quarter after two. The clock on the tank had stopped again.

I found a couple guys sitting on a picnic bench and asked them which of the two restaurants would have a good cheap cheeseburger. They pointed at the diner-looking place. Nice little mom-and-pop joint. The place was empty. Pop came out with a menu and water. I ordered quick and ducked back to the bathroom to run some cold water over my head.

When I finished my burger the guys were still sitting on the bench out front. I crossed the lot and lit a cigarette. Rosinante had cooled off quite a bit. Her engine was still hot enough, and her chain hung a little limp. Another hundred miles and I'd lose my shit along the I-5 freeway. I hunkered down on the curb. "Now what, Rosi?" As if she'd have some sort of answer. I finished that cigarette and another, watching parking lot traffic slide past.

A beat-up Toyota pickup lurched across the lot, around to the end, and jerked toward me. I thought about getting up, or getting out of the way, but he hadn't really hit anything yet. He jerked into a parking spot next to Rosinante. The two guys from the front of the restaurant got out, stretched like they'd crossed the country, and tugged at a tarp in the truck bed. One of the guys nodded at me. They pulled down the gate, slid a cooler out from under the tarp, and pulled out a couple cans of cold beer. "Hey buddy," one of the guys called over. "Hey, you want a beer?" he asked.

I wasn't sure if he was talking to me. "Sure," I said.

He brought me a can of beer. "What's wrong with it?"

"She's vaporlocked and the chain's slack." I cracked my beer and took a long pull. "Thanks."

He nodded and sat on the curb next to me. "So you going to fix it?" he asked.

"Left my tools in my saddlebag." I shrugged. "I'm fucked."

"Somebody coming to help you?" he asked.

"Just got to find a couple of wrenches and I'll be good again."

"We're waiting for his tools," he told me. "He's got wrenches."

The other guy was a bit bigger, but looked about the same. They could be brothers. Big guy leaned against the fender of the truck. "I let my friend install a cable, but he put it in backwards. Now I gotta fix it again in the damn parking lot."

"That sucks," I said.

"My roommate is going to get my tools from the house and bring them here." He shrugged and spit. "We were supposed to be on our way to the lake to go camping."

"That sucks."

"Try to call him again," the guy on the curb said.

"I did. He's still not answering."

"What a fuckin' asshole," he muttered.

The guy leaning against the truck pulled his cellphone out of the cab and looked at the screen.

"Did he call?"

"Not yet."

"Well call him."

"He's still not answering, man. He's not going to answer, alright?"

"Fuck." He drained the rest of his beer, crumpled his can and tossed it over his shoulder. "You guys ready for another?" He brought back three beers. We chugged ours.

The guy sat on the curb again and dug into his pocket. "You smoke pot?" he asked.

"When I've got it."

"You wanna smoke some now?"

You sure can pick a rescue team, Rosi. "Sure, why not."

He pulled a pipe from his shirt pocket and packed a bowl. Of all the places to break down, this place wasn't too bad. At least the natives were friendly.

We smoked a bowl and sat around, picking up handfuls of pebbles and flicking them across the lot.

"Call him again," the one guy said.

"I told you, he's not answering. I'm wasting my batteries."

"Maybe he'll answer this time."

The guy dialed the phone. He held it to his ear. After a minute or so he rubbed his face. "Pick up the fucking phone for fuck's sake!" he yelled into the earpiece.

"Is he there?"

"What do you think?" He squatted down against the tire.

"Damn," the guy on the curb said, looking off towards the street.

"What?"

He pointed toward the street. An old Honda Civic turned into the lot. "It's Gina." He smiled.

"Hot damn." The other guy smiled.

The Honda rolled into the lot indecisively. When Gina spotted the boys, she turned down the lane and pulled into the parking spot right next to the truck. Gina got out. She was hot, wearing a pair of tight jeans and a little tanktop. "I thought you boys were going camping." She stood with her arms folded across her chest and her hip cocked to the side.

"Truck's fucked," the big guy said.

"We're stuck," the other guy said.

"So you're just going to sit here drinking beer?" she asked.

"Waiting for tools," The big guy told her.

The guy on the curb reached into his pocket. "You want to smoke some pot?" He pulled the pipe out, stacked it, and held it out to her.

She thought about it for a moment. "Yeah, what the hell." She took the pipe and leaned against the fender to smoke it. "Who's bringing the tools?" she asked.

"Roommate," the big guy said.

"Well where is he?"

"Fuck if I know," he said. "He's not answering his phone."

"Fuckin' asshole." The other guy grunted through a puff of smoke.

"Who's he?" Gina pointed at me.

"I'm Aaron." I waved.

"He's fucked too," the big guy said.

She nodded. "You going camping?" she asked me.

"If I don't fix my chain I might." I smiled.

"Where the fuck is he?" The big guy spat and paced to the end of the truck for another beer. He brought three more back with him and passed them out.

"Does he have your tools with him?" Gina asked.

"Nah, they're at my house. He has to go get them."

"Why don't you call somebody else?"

"He has a key."

She took a drink. "Well I can go get them." She shrugged. Gina was getting hotter by the minute.

The big guy pulled his keys from his pocket and handed them to her. "The toolbox is just inside the door."

Gina finished the rest of her beer, got back in her car and sped away.

"Thank god for Gina," the big guy said.

"Fuck yeah," the other guy said. He repacked the pipe and we passed it around again.

By the time Gina got back I was well baked, and had a decent buzz going. She pulled up right behind the pickup truck and popped her trunk. "Damn that thing is heavy," she said.

The big guy lifted the toolbox out of the trunk and lugged it up alongside the truck. "Damn, Gina," he said. "You saved my ass."

"I know." She checked her phone. "I'm late. Tell your sister to call me." She jumped back in her car and took off again.

The big guy popped the latch on the box and rifled through the top tray. "What do you need?" he asked.

"A couple of adjustable wrenches."

He pulled two out and handed them to me.

I squatted down at the back tire. In a few minutes I had the chain tightened.

The big guy was under his truck, cranking away at a bolt.

"Where you headed?" the other guy asked. He sat on the asphalt between the two vehicles.

"Home." I said.

"Where's home?" he asked.

"Wherever Habibi is."

"You going to see a girl?"

"*The* girl." I smiled.

He nodded. "Right on." He dug into his pocket again. "Wanna smoke a bowl before you go?"

Hell of a rescue team you found us, Rosinante. “Sure.”

We smoked one last bowl while I pulled on my leather and checked the straps on the bag. As I was pulling on my helmet the big guy’s phone rang.

“Where the fuck have you been?” he demanded.

I buckled my helmet on and walked the bike backward.

“I been waiting all afternoon,” he said.

I saluted the other guy and walked Rosinante out a bit.

The other guy saluted back. Big guy under the truck waved. “What the fuck good is the cellphone if you don’t fuckin’ pick it up?” he said.

I zipped up my jacket.

“Well not now. I already fixed it,” he said.

When I started her up, Rosinante sounded just fine. I kicked Rosinante down to first. She idled easy. I rolled on a little throttle. She sputtered and popped and jerked toward the exit. Big guy worked under his truck. The other guy squatted down next to him and offered him the pipe.

Rosinante was still a little rough. It took a mile at twenty before the fuel kicked in, and then she was as good as ever. I followed Main Street back through the rows of trees, hung a right on 99, and kicked her up a gear. By the time we hit the onramp, we were pulling seventy easy, and I popped her up into third, clawing my way back up to speed.

Burnt

I could see the smoke in my rearview. After a few miles, I decided that it was coming from Rosinante's tail, and that it was a good time to take a break. I rolled off the 5 at the next truck stop. Found a coffee shop. I wasn't in much better shape than Rosinante, worn out in my neck and back, but I was getting used to it. Took a few minutes to dig my spiral out of the bag. My hands were burnt beyond sunscreen.

The place just reeked of off-ramp. Bikers and truckers, mostly truckers. At least no strip mall. I found a spot at the counter and flipped my spiral open to the next page. A thin, feminine guy with dark hair dropped off silverware and a menu and eyed the blond streak in my hair. I guess it probably did look sort of gay. A few minutes later, a spent-looking bleach blonde leaned against the counter with her coffee pot ready. I nodded and flipped my mug. "Hungry?" she asked.

"Mind if I just sit here a while?"

"Sure, hon." She filled my mug. "Cream?" She pulled a couple of creamers out from under the counter.

"Black's fine."

She dropped the creamers back under the counter and glanced at my helmet. "What kind of bike?"

"EX500."

"That's one of them Jap bikes." She set the pot back on the burner. "My ex rode a Harley."

"Can't afford one. Fuckin' weekend warriors drove the price up."

She smiled. Crow's foot crevices formed in her makeup. "That's why he's my ex."

I guess I could afford one if I wanted it bad enough to settle for the five years it would take to pay the damn thing off. Obsess on the chrome. Polish it with a diaper. But it'd be worth it to get that American-born sticker, right?

Guy on my left was wearing a meshback trucker hat. No neck. His beard ran a sharp angle into chest hair. He and his friend were laughing. I stared at the page. I was trying to explain to the girl that I really did love her, that her anger was making it hard to work up the sort of lovesick righteousness that I needed to keep rolling. The meshback and his friend kept glancing over at my helmet and cracking jokes. Finally, he leaned over. "What is that shit on your helmet. That sand nigger writing?"

"Same as on his motorcycle." His friend hooked a finger over his shoulder.

"It's Arabic," I said, without looking up.

"Yeah, A-rabic." He elbowed his friend. "Well, what's it say?"

I was sorry that I hadn't learned a single cuss word in Arabic yet. "It says Habibi."

"What's that?"

"That like a Commie?" the other guy asked.

I wanted to tell him that she was very much like a commie, like my dearest Commie love. I wanted to tell him all about her, every graphic detail, from her eyes at first glance to our sweat drying on her naked breasts. I wanted him to understand her kiss when we last parted and the misery ever since. I thought about grabbing him by his flannel collars and rattling his fat face like a bobble-head dashboard toy. I thought about spitting love lyrics at him, laughing and kicking his chicken-fried steak down his fucking throat so far that he and his whole inbred family tree choked on his stupidity. I wanted to explain love so that he might understand it as I understood it, as the fearsome and dangerous power that compelled me to destroy anyone and everything that stood between me and my lover, including, but not limited to, stupid, fat hillbillies. I wanted to, but that would take time, and time was something that I didn't have enough of anymore. "It means 'my lover,'" I said.

"Sand nigger lover," his friend muttered.

"Camel lover," the meshback laughed.

I folded my spiral closed and stuffed it back into my pack. The waitress watched, concerned, and eyed the huge black man a few seats down. He had stopped eating and stared down the counter at the lot of us. I pulled a couple of dollars from my pocket to offer her, but she waved me off. "I got it, hon," she said. I nodded my thanks.

"You a camel fucker?" the meshback asked. His friend laughed.

I pulled my leather on. As I was pulling on my pack, the shoulder strap caught on the corner of the American flag patch. The wind had been peeling back the iron on glue for a few hours. I yanked the patch off and picked up my helmet. As I walked past, they were still laughing. His friend cringed slightly when I tossed the patch into the middle of the meshback's plate.

"Go back to the Al-Kay-da, Camel Fucker." his friend said.

They were quiet for just a second and then laughed at something else. I heard a piece of silverware hit the counter and a stool scoot across the linoleum. The big guy at the end of the bar stood up and wiped his mouth with his napkin.

The bell above the door rang as I stepped out.

Rosinante was still hot, but she wasn't smoking so bad. I figured if I could make it another fifteen miles, I was bound to find someplace else to rest. I checked all the straps and pulled on my helmet. The sunburn was turning the backs of my hands leathery.

Through the front window, I watched the big guy fold his arms across his chest like a load of lumber he was waiting to unload. Meshback and his buddy stayed seated, both of them leaning back a little. Meshback was saying something, but the big guy wasn't moving. I backed out, pushed the button, and Rosinante sputtered back, throaty and obviously tired. We pulled back onto the 5 and hit ninety-five almost instantly, sliding out into the left lane and as fast and far away as I could.

A few minutes later, a state patrol raced past on the opposite side of the barricade, sirens flashing, and headed, I hoped, for a call about an ass-kicking at the truck stop lunch counter. The strange thing is, it took a couple of assholes to work me back into that righteous sort of angelic state, but I had enough MOAB in me to get me another couple hundred miles at least.

Fields white with clover

Another hour down the road, I was well past worn. The muscles were twisted and knotted so tight in my back and neck that I couldn't turn my head without hissing into my helmet. A couple of rest stop signs gave me hope, and the exit arched off into grass and trees and a breezy alternative to choking the hell out of the next fucker to open his mouth. I stripped my armor, hung my jacket on the handlebars, stretched, did a couple of pushups, and walked over to take a leak. The sprinklers came on just as I stepped out of the bathroom, so I took a walk around the lawn, soaking myself to the skin and dug through my pocket to find a cigarette. An old man leaned against the front of a greyed VW campervan a few parking spots down. The roof was covered in a variety of antennae and dishes, and a strange apparatus was bolted to the side, some sort of external radiator, I guessed. The man had a long, grey beard, frizzy grey hair, and a golf cap tilted funny on his head. His laugh revealed a few missing teeth. "Hotter than hell today." He smiled.

I nodded.

"You'll be dry again in a few minutes, I bet."

"Yup."

He stood up, stretched his twiggy arms, and yawned. "You got another one of those?"

"Sure."

"Supposed to be quitting and all, but…"

"Yeah, me too." He took a smoke and nodded, waited for a light.

He glanced back at the motorcycle, squinted through his own puff, and waved the smoke out of the way. "Your bike's smoking, you know?"

"Yeah. She just took up the habit."

"Hard ride?"

"Hard enough."

"Where you headed?"

"North."

"Someplace important, I bet."

"Girl."

He laughed and nodded.

"Well, what are you doing out here?"

"Out?"

"Travelling?"

"Ah shoot." He pulled off his cap and dusted at the bill. "I'm hiding out from my old lady." And he hung his cap on the rearview mirror. "Been married forty-seven years next October." He glanced off. "She likes me gone these days." He leaned in, "Keeps her kitchen cleaner, I suppose." He gave me a wink and a gap-toothed grin. We both laughed.

He walked over to the edge of the grass and held his hands out to catch the edge of the spray. When his palms were sufficiently wet, he smoothed the mess of hair back over the thin spot at the back of his head. The cigarette hung from his lips and he squinted out toward the highway. "I suppose I won't be at this much longer." He scowled.

"Miss her?"

He smiled softly and nodded. "Not that I'd let her know."

"Forty-seven years. That's a whole lifetime."

He nodded. "We're getting along, these days. Can't do it like we used to."

I wasn't exactly sure what to tell him, console him or congratulate him. I imagined his septuagenarian wife somewhere with her tits around her waist and a rolling pin like a club, chasing him out of her kitchen. Not doing it like they used to could be a good thing.

"Doc diagnosed her with Alzheimer's last winter," he said.

"I'm sorry."

"Ah, she's been senile for the past thirty years. Now at least she's got a good excuse for forgetting her keys somewhere."

I smiled.

He dragged sharply at his smoke and smacked his lips like it was a cigar. "And contrary to what anyone tells you, she may forget her glasses, her keys, her name and mine, but she'll never forget a single time I screwed up. I promise you that." He chuckled.

Fuel

We eased up the off-ramp and coasted into a Chevron, straight up to pump one. I pulled the key and popped her gas cap. She leaned against her kickstand, smoking. Her oil was low and dark again.

The gas station was air-conditioned, felt like a walk-in cooler on my extra crispy skin. I wanted to strip naked and roll around on the linoleum until the last of the heat exhaustion left my body. I wanted to, but I figured that might be a good way to make people nervous about me. I picked up a quart of oil and a Butterfinger and walked up to the girl behind the counter.

Her nametag said Ginny, with a smiley-face sticker and some sort of award button pinned to it. She was a heavy blonde with a little-girl face set above a disturbing amount of cleavage. She smiled and rang me up. I put a few bucks on the pump. Her manager stood behind her, a tall guy, thinning hair combed over his balding pate.

"When does it start to cool down around here?" I asked.

Ginny glanced up at the manager, deferring to a professional opinion. "September," the manager said.

"Does it cool down at night?"

"A couple degrees."

Ginny stepped out the front door with a Marlboro Ultra Light 100 between her fingers. She made a big show of patting her pockets and proving she had no lighter. She looked as casual as she could, walking over to me with cigarette poised. "Can I borrow your light?" She cocked her hip. Gotta love a small-town girl. They're easy reads.

I fished my lighter out and lit her smoke. Stared off across the street with my eyes all squinty like her rebel-whatever fantasy ought to.

"That your bike?"

I glanced over at the still smoking Rosi. "Yup."

"What kinda bike?"

Maybe I should just say Harley. "She used to be an EX500."

She nodded like she'd read the Chilton's Manual on Kawasakis. "Kinda rusty," she said.

"She likes the rain."

She gave me a token smile. "Where you headed?"

"Home."

"Where's home?"

"Washington."

"Long ride."

I glanced up at the freeway onramp sign, sort of smirking. "Yup." This rebel thing was getting easy.

A pale blue, mid-eighties Ford station wagon bounced into the lot. Ginny ashed her cigarette and glanced over her shoulder as she spoke. "That's my dad." He pulled up and parked in front of us. The guy behind the wheel was thin and weathered. Mid-fifties at least, but worn. Three little blond heads bobbed in the seats around him. I might have guessed they were Ginny's kids, but even if she started at a freakishly early age, there were a couple in there that were eight or nine at least, and Ginny couldn't be more than seventeen.

"Whose kids?"

"His." As the car doors opened, Ginny stepped forward and said hello. She ushered the kids out of the back seat and helped herd them along behind her dad. He looked old enough to be their grandfather, but they tugged at his shirt and followed close behind him. She came back to stand beside me and watched him inside. "His wife was only ten years older than me," she said. "But after Eric was born, she got breast cancer and died." Ginny put out her smoke and smiled. "Well, good luck," she chirped.

I tried to imagine what it would be like to be a sixty-year-old guy running around with three kids. The man just looked haggard. He came out of the store followed by the three, walked them across to the car, and opened the door for them. He glanced over the bike, and gave me a good stern check.

"You serve?" He pointed to the shoulder of my jacket. A pale striped scar remained where I'd torn the flag patch off.

I thought about lying, just in case. "No," I said.

"Hmm." He nodded. He was a harder read than his daughter. Could go either way.

"A couple guys called me a camel fucker a few stops back." I shrugged. "Didn't feel so patriotic anymore."

He nodded, fished a pack of Parliaments from his pocket, and pulled out a smoke.

"Did you serve?" I asked.

He packed the cigarette against the back of his watch and shook his head. His eyes were grey slits, staring off toward the west. He lit the cigarette and took a long drag, doing a gristled Henry Fonda in a threadbare denim shirt. "Which way you headed?" he asked.

I felt like lying again, just in case he was ready to call Homeland Security. "North," I said.

He nodded. "How far?"

"Eastern Washington." I cracked my neck and rolled it as I took the next drag.

He smiled. It caught me off guard.

He nodded, glanced back at the bike. "Head gasket's fucked," he said.

"I figured."

"Might not make it over the pass."

"I've got to."

He nodded. "You keeping it in oil?"

I nodded.

"That's about all you can do."

The easy onset of Nighttime

Mount Shasta was pure pleasure. Pines peppered the foothills, appearing in clumps and clusters at first, then rising sharply into jagged, green walls to the left and treetops to the right. I got to daydreaming that if I hard charged the next curve, I might get a good fifty feet out before Rosi and I dropped into the ravine. I pushed the throttle as the road got steep. Rosinante strained at ninety. We eased back to eighty and seventy and sixty and fifty. I dropped into second gear to meander past the truckers crawling along at thirty and less. One-and-a-half cylinders. Better than the Lazarus mount, at least.

Gas stations on the mountain were running from $3.95 a gallon on up. I pulled off to rest a minute and try the payphone. Rosinante was low, but I couldn't justify putting more than a gallon into her. I bought some gas, smokes, and a Drumstick ice cream cone. I tried using the calling card, but it didn't have enough minutes left to make another call.

She decide to love you again, or what?

"You know what they say, if you love something, set it free. If it comes back, it was always yours."

They're fullacrap. If you love something, put it in a big box, bury it deep, and kill anybody that knows where you hid it. That's the only way.

"You can't bury Habibi in a box."

Well, put some air holes in it or something.

Bubblegum, petcocks, and pop culture

I started smelling gasoline long before I was past Shasta. A hundred or so miles from the pass and not quite halfway home. I ran my fingers along the edge of the tank and found it dripping, my left pant leg damp. I passed my fingers under the helmet for a sniff in case it was condensation, but we knew it wasn't.

It's coming and it's not far behind.

I checked the rearview mirror. There were no flames. No headlights, even. Just highway and a few minutes ago. I only wish I could get warm. I pulled off at the next exit, not much more than a few fast-food joints and a gas station. I pulled into a parking lot and hopped off the bike. Pulled off my helmet and inspected the petcock. It dripped against the engine case and frame.

"Fuck," I said.

The world's about to come to an end anyway. Let's just steal a car or something.

"I'm still not seeing how you're getting pirates out of all this."

Fuck do you care, dipshit?

"I gotta listen to this shit, too."

Yeah? Alright, monkey. Bin Laden blows up a couple of buildings and hides out in Afghanistan, so the President invades Iraq. The man talks Jihad, but he starts a holy war in Jesus' name, amen, and his watchword is Wrath. The term 'Shock and Awe' comes to mean desensitized, 'mission accomplished' means we're in this forever, the government is blowing trillions of dollars each year on a neverending war, and instead of rioting in the streets, you talk about putting back together a damn rusted-out turdboiler of a bike, just so you can run back to your next perfect little piece of ass. You hole yerself up in a basement and hide out. You talk about action, and yet, you get none. Any of this make sense? You feeling like a pirate yet?

"She's not a piece of ass."

I rest my case.

"She is not my next perfect little piece of ass, damnit!"

You're yelling at an empty parking lot.

"Hey man, what year's your Ducati?" The sound of another voice was unnerving somehow. There was a kid standing a few feet back.

"It's not a Ducati."

"What is it?" He was a skinny kid with spikey blond hair and a baby face, wearing a hoodie sweatshirt, baggy jeans, and sneakers. In one hand, he had a skateboard, in the other, a can of Rockstar energy drink. He took a sip from his can and squinted at me.

Tell him, Noskivvies muttered.

"It's an EX500," I said. "A Kawasaki."

"Oh." He spit at the parking lot.

Tell him it's your horse.

He took another long gulp of the Rockstar. "It sounds like a Ducati," he said, like I was lying.

"Pipes are rusted," I said.

Tell him that you're the fifth horseman of the apocalypse. Death on steel. Tell him that you're six hundred miles to ground zero and the biggest mushroom cloud since Hiroshima. Tell him that everything is gonna end soon. Tell him that you're the MOAB.

The kid blew a bubble. It popped.

Fuck it, just get rid of him.

"What kinda gum is that?" I asked.

"Bubblegum."

"Got anymore?"

"Whole pack." He reached in his pocket and pulled out a pack of gum, showed it to me, and put it back.

"Give ya a buck for the rest," I said.

You're such a waste.

"Sure." He dug the pack out of his pocket. I handed him a dollar. "Sucker." He laughed. "There's a Sevvy around the corner. Coulda bought a pack there cheaper."

I pulled out a piece, chewed like mad. I figured I'd have to get the last of the sugar out before it was any good to me. I held one out to the kid. "Gimme the one you're chewing."

"What?"

"I gotta patch my tank."

He laughed. "Whatever." He pulled the piece from his mouth and handed it to me.

"I'll give you another buck if you'll help me chew the flavor outta this whole pack." I stuck the gum to Rosi's windshield

He didn't seem too sure at first, but he put the next piece in his mouth, glancing over the bike. "What happened to that thing? Get in an accident or what?"

Tell him we're the fucking MOAB.

"No," I said.

"How'd it get so jacked?"

"Rain rusted it out." I shrugged. "And it got run over twice."

"Twice?" He shook his head and whistled. "Maybe you oughta get a new one."

"Less yackin', more chewin'."

"Hey Jeff!" he hollered. "C'mere!" Another kid rode off the curb, rolling across the lot on a skateboard. "He's gonna fix it with gum!"

"No shit?"

I handed Jeff the pack as he rolled up. "Chew."

"Sad," he mumbled, unwrapping a piece, "I thought it was a monster."

"Don't let the paint job fool ya. It is."

I unstrapped the knapsack, pulled the seat, and set to unbolting the tank, cranking the makeshift bolt by hand.

Jeff chomped at the gum. "You think gum will hold it?"

"For a few miles at least," I said.

"How far are you going?"

"Farther than that," I said.

"Yer fucked, man," the first kid said.

"Just chew."

After cranking at the bolt for a few minutes, it finally gave enough to get it turning. I flipped the petcock valve and yanked the fuel lines. Gas dripped on the frame and a bit trickled. I laid it gently against the curb. There wasn't enough fuel in the tank to leak out the cap. Digging through the knapsack I pulled out a T-shirt and wiped the excess fuel from around the petcock. I could see the hole. It wasn't much more than a speck, but enough to piss fuel, I guess. Jeff and the other kid sat on the curb, chomping and watching.

"So what are you guys doing out so late?" I asked.

They glanced at each other and shrugged. "Hangin' out."

"Your folks let you stay out this late?"

"Fuck are they gonna do about it?" the first kid asked.

"You guys don't have school or something tomorrow?"

"It's the weekend," Jeff said.

I was losing days. How long had I been out? A week, two weeks, maybe. I guess I lost track back at the cabin. We couldn't have been up there for more than a few days, but it seemed like weeks. As I was trying to count sleepless nights, Jeff pulled the gum out of his mouth and stuck it to the wad on Rosinante's windshield. He pulled another piece from the pack, unwrapped it, and started chewing again.

"Did you call Lisa?" Jeff asked the other kid.

He nodded.

"What's she doing?"

"Grounded." the other kid snarled.

Jeff laughed. "Last night?"

The kid nodded. "Her dad took a swing at me."

"No shit?"

"He was in the kitchen when I tried to make a break for it. Caught me trying to run out the sliding glass door."

"Did he hit you? You could probably sue."

"That fat fuck's slow as shit."

"Bet you're glad your folks put you in karate instead of Boy Scouts."

He laughed. "Kung fu, man." He chomped a couple of times and pulled the wad out of his mouth, glanced at it, and put it back in his mouth. "If that fucker laid a hand on me, I could snap every tendon in his fuckin' wrist."

"Sure, dude. You're gonna fuck up Coach Randall."

"Fuck yeah I could. It's easy. I could make it look like it was an accident even."

"Right."

"Seriously, catch his wrist and fall on it. Tendons'd snap like old rubber bands."

Jeff laughed. "Whatever."

The kid pulled the wad out of his mouth and pushed it into the lump on the windshield. "Anyway, I didn't have to." He took a few gulps from his Rockstar and pulled another piece from the pack. "Hey man, you seriously need us to chew this whole pack?"

I pulled the piece from my mouth and stuck it to the wad on the windshield. "You want your buck, keep chewing."

He snorted and pulled another piece from the pack. "My jaw's starting to hurt."

I shrugged. "I could look up Coach Randall and tell him where you're at."

He gave me the finger. "I could light a fuckin' match, asshole."

I smiled. "You're almost done."

He stuffed another piece in his mouth and started chewing. Jeff pulled the piece out of his mouth and looked at it. He put it back in his mouth and started chewing again. "So?" he asked.

"So what?" the kid said.

"So what about Lisa?"

"I told you, she's grounded now."

"No, I mean how far'dju get?"

The kid smiled and chomped.

"You touch a titty?"

He snorted and leaned back.

"What?"

"Got my digits in her axe wound." He nodded.

"No shit?"

The kid nodded.

"You did what?" I asked.

The kid rolled his eyes at Jeff and glanced over at me, looking annoyed. "I got my fingers in her twat."

"How old are you?" I asked.

"Fourteen. Why, you got a problem with that, too?"

"Nah, kid." I checked the petcock to see how dry it was. "Just never heard anybody call it an axe wound before."

"You a faggot?" He leaned forward.

"Yeah. I'm a big, ol' fuckin' faggot. Just chew."

Jeff pulled his piece out and pushed it into the wad. "That's it, man, you're outta gum."

The petcock was dry enough. I spit in my hand and pulled the wad from the windshield, kneading it in my palm.

"It ain't gonna hold, man," the kid said.

"It'll hold for a few miles, at least."

"And then what?"

"I don't know. I'll try not to drive near an open flame, I guess."

The collection of gum was already hardening, but it softened as I warmed it and kneaded it. The kid pulled the wad from his mouth and pushed it into the pink lump. I spit on it again and kept working it. Where it dried, it got sticky, and I was hopeful. Faith alone, right? I pressed the gum into the pinhole, kneading it to get it as deep as possible. Jeff and the kid sat there watching.

"There's no fucking way, man," the kid said. "Gas eats through plastic."

"Maybe it'll hold for a hundred miles or so."

"Not likely."

Get rid of him, damnit.

"I don't know," Jeff said. "Mom said gum can sit in your intestines for a couple years, and that's acidic, right? Who knows? It might make it."

"Thank you," I said. "That's what I'm relying on."

"No fuckin' way," the kid said. "Gas'll turn a styrofoam cup to goo in like half a minute. There's no way gum could hold it."

"Yeah, well, you guys made a couple bucks at least, right?" I kneaded the gum around the petcock, coating the outside. I got most of it coated and pressed it around the edges, working the seam together and sculpting a rubbery pink coating. When I was satisfied that it was going to stick to itself, I stood up and stretched my legs, wiping the last of the spit on my jeans.

"There's no way," the kid said.

Alright. That's it.

I pulled out a cigarette and my lighter.

The kid jumped up and back a few feet. "What the fuck are you doing?"

I held the lighter poised at the end of the cigarette, ready to light. "What the fuck does it look like?"

"Dude, can you smell the gasoline? You're gonna blow us all up!"

Jeff stood up.

"Saves me a few hundred miles," I said.

The kid grabbed Jeff's shirt and yanked him back. "Dude. Yer fuckin' crazy, man."

I smiled and shrugged. "Not dead yet." I flicked the lighter.

The kid cringed and covered his face.

Nothing exploded. I lit my smoke and smiled at Jeff.

Jeff smiled. "I think it's gonna work."

I winked. "Worth a shot at least, huh?"

He nodded.

I reached into my pocket to dig out a couple of bucks and walked toward them.

The kid kept walking backward, and almost tripped over a bush. "Back the fuck off, man!" He took a kung fu posture.

"You gonna snap my tendons now, kid?"

He clenched his fists and flexed like his skinny fourteen-year-old frame might make me think twice.

"Alright, kid. I'll see your fu, and I'll raise you the *lengua del diablo*." I unzipped the knapsack and pulled out the little water bottle full of lamp oil. "You know what a MOAB is?" I pulled on my left glove.

The kid didn't move. I poured a little lamp oil in the palm of the glove and let the puddle warm, holding it out in front of me. "It's the Mother Of All Bombs, the largest non-nuclear bomb we have in the American arsenal; a fuel-air mixture. It drops over a city, opening several hundred feet above the ground. The fuel inside atomizes - do you know what that means? - It means that it spreads out into tiny droplets, like rain. A few hundred feet above the ground, the ignition switch goes, and the fuel catches, raining fire on everything below it. Burns every living thing to a crisp. People, pets, you, me, Lisa, and Coach Randall, wallowing in flames," I said.

"You're fucking crazy, man," the kid said. His jaw was clenched.

I smiled. "I am the MOAB, kid." I pulled a swig of lamp oil into my mouth, set the bottle down, and flicked my lighter into my palm. The lamp oil caught and for all intents and purposes, it looked like I just set fire to a handful of water. I held my flaming palm out and spit an aerosol fine spray at it. A fifteen foot long fireball exploded upward, spreading out like dragon's breath against the night sky. The kid staggered backward into the street. I spit a couple of little fireballs, just to clear my mouth, and held my flaming palm out to him. The kid looked ready to piss his pants.

"Holy shit!" Jeff laughed. "How'd you do that?"

I spit the last of the fuel away and patted my glove out on my jacket. "I told you. I'm the MOAB." I smiled.

"Ah fuck." The kid was up and moving backward. He turned and started running. "I'm calling the fucking cops, you asshole!" he screamed over his shoulder. Chances were good that if anybody else saw that, they were already on the phone.

"How'd you do that?" Jeff asked again.

I laughed. "Magic." I wiped the rest of my palm clean and picked up my cigarette and lamp oil, stuffing the latter back into my knapsack.

"No, seriously, you gotta show me that."

"I gotta get outta here before that kid calls the cops." I picked up the gas tank and slid it back into place, tightening the bolt back as quick as I could. I tightened the bungees, pulled my jacket back on, zipped up, pulled my helmet off the handlebars, and flicked my cigarette away. It spiraled out into the street. "You want your buck or not?" I pulled on my helmet and buckled it.

He shook his head, still bewildered. "Keep it, man. That was awesome."

I pulled on my gloves and flipped the key. Rosi's console lights turned on.

"Who are you?" he asked, standing right beside me.

"I told ya. I'm the fucking MOAB." I flipped the petcock valve on. "Am I leaking yet?"

"What?"

I pointed at the bubble-gummed valve.

He glanced down. "No."

I nodded and pushed the start button. Rosinante rumbled back to life, her headlight spilling out over the empty parking lot.

"Where are you going?"

"HOME!" I hollered over her engine. I saluted and kicked her down to first. Rolling on the throttle, she hopped up for a few feet and rolled around toward the street. Jeff stood in the middle of the lot, arms limp at his sides. Maybe that was all I needed, one kid to believe I was superhuman, one kid to know that I was going to make it home. As I hit the street I jumped gears up to fourth, hit the onramp doing sixty. *Faster, Rosinante.*

I gunned it up to ninety to put in some distance. All I needed was a little momentum and a nice long stretch to crash land.

Video game

There was one long, white line to my left and a dashed yellow to my right, reflectors rolled a solid glowing bass beat. In the distance, there were pairs of white and red lights and they all swam past eventually. There wasn't much moon to speak of. The night sky was clear and black, stars bright enough to light the sky but little else. There was no world outside Rosinante's headlights. The Yoshi pipe buzzed in my skull in a long and perfect Om. In the low valleys, the air was moist, and I could smell water. Sometimes there were bugs. Sometimes there were clouds of gnats. For a few miles, the freeway was soft curves and long smooth stretches. At last, I understood why Q called it her video game. Armored and isolated by little more than leather, my flesh was made metal, the throaty roar of an engine working against the back of my skull. The light bounced and glided ahead. I leaned and we rolled. Sometimes we hit a roll just right and got light. I slowed to seventy and sat up to let the wind hit my chest. The grasslands were lush but sort of monochromatic compared to the soft rhythmic glow of those lines.

I wanted to believe that there was a happy ending a few hundred miles away, but I couldn't be sure. Habibi was still on radio silence. I still couldn't get her on the phone, and the last time we spoke it was a little less like romance than a prize fight.

Happy endings are a myth, monkey.

Oh yes, and then there was the fucking Cap'n, who wasn't helping things much.

"We could have gotten arrested back there," I said.

Tell me you didn't love the look on that kid's face as he ran off.

A few miles ahead, a pair of taillights swam across the freeway, sliding from one side to the other. As we crept up on them, I got the feeling like maybe the driver had no idea how drunk he was. The truck swerved across two lanes, rattled on the reflectors for a moment and swerved back again.

"This guy's going to kill himself."

Long as he doesn't get us killed.

As we got closer the lights became an old Chevrolet pickup truck, green and rusted out. Must be late seventies or so, something big and lumbering, deadly if I got too close. I slowed and dropped a gear, drafting about twenty feet behind him. There were two silhouettes in the cab, both smoking out of the windows. On occasion, when they flicked ash, glowing orange stardust fell away from the sides of the truck. I reached down and touched the petcock. The fingertips of the glove came back damp and smelling of gasoline. "So much for the bubblegum fix." I edged up in the passing lane, hanging beside the left margin. As I closed the gap, the truck slid to the right and clung to his lane. At least he saw me. Rosinante crept forward. As we got close, though, he drifted left again, the back bumper crossing the center line a couple of feet away. I rolled off the throttle and backed down. "Fuck."

We slow down anymore and maybe you can get off and walk this thing past him, huh?

We were down to fifty miles per hour. His passenger watched me out the back window. I could see him laughing. *These guys are fucking with us.*

The truck hung between the lanes, splitting them and coasting steady. The driver flicked his cigarette away. A glowing ember floated, caught the wind, and sailed back at us. I swerved to the right and hung in the slow lane as the butt bounced and shattered to glowing orange glitter in my rearview mirror.

Yeah! Bring it on, motherfucker! Noskivvies edged forward. *Now this is what I call adventure.* He leaned on the throttle.

"Knock it off, man. We're gonna die out here."

Big fuckin' deal. Everybody dies.

"Yeah, well, I'd rather not do it now. Not here."

Why not? You think maybe it'll be nice to die in bed sixty years from now? You know, we hit one of those butts just right, and this whole thing might be over real soon. How's this for a happy ending: You, me, and this rusted-out nag turn fiery ball of flames at seventy miles per hour. Now that's fucking romantic, yeah? They can mail your lovelorn ashes back to Habibi in a matchbox. Shit, you hit it just right, and they can name a few miles of asphalt after you.

We were thirty feet behind the truck, rolling along at an easy pace. The driver lit another cigarette and straddled the lanes. For a man who couldn't stick a lane a few miles back, he was doing a great job of sticking both now.

I say we're done. He rolled on the throttle and we coasted up along the centerline, pulling straight in behind the truck. It swerved a little, but held the line. As we crept up on the back bumper, they hit the brakes. We faked right and swerved left, dropped it into third and opened the throttle. As we sailed past the driver, the truck rattled over the trucker grooves on the right side. In a few seconds, we were clear and doing an easy ninety.

Yeah bitches! Full speed ahead and damn the torpedoes!

I began to wonder if we weren't all on the brink of that apocryphal apocalypse. Like the whole of humanity was packed into a rollercoaster car, getting up to the top of the first big drop. We were all about to go over the edge and no one wanted to talk about it, so they ignored the tick tick tick … tick … tick … tick…

But we were already off, losing bodies all over the place because the ride wasn't rated for seven billion people.

It was supposed to be a rambling ride up the coast, getting in touch with the country that I lost a couple of years ago. Instead, I found *nothing* but parking lots, mini-malls, prejudice, and decadence. The land of the free and the home of the brave was replaced by a mindless consumer culture; adults reveling in their ignorance, and kids who didn't even know they got fucked the first time their mother dropped them in front of a television.

Yer one to talk.

"This is bullshit, man."

At long last, yer getting' it.

We laughed.

Oasis Kiss

The next rest stop was Klamath River, just a few miles south of the Oregon-California border. The lot was set off the freeway by a few hundred yards, nestled into the river valley. The rest stop had a nice, big picnic area with a few fir trees. Beyond the picnic tables and bathrooms, the lawn sloped down to the river.

I parked Rosinante under a lamp post, yanked the seat off, and pulled the tank. When I tilted it at the right angle, the gas stopped leaking. The bubblegum was gone. *Nothing* was left of it. It must have melted away. As I looked it over, I puffed cautiously at part of a joint. I started to get cold, so I pulled on another sweater.

Habibi and I stopped there on the drive down. We slept in the back of the truck, ate blackberries off the vine in the morning, and stood in the river in our bathing suits, using some hippy soap to take a quick bath. I smoked a cigarette looking down at the river, thinking of her. The moonlight couldn't penetrate the tree branches, and so it lay shattered across the surface of the river. The water was dark, cold, and swift. From the edge of where I stood, the shadows flowed south, little but the dim impression of something big moving just out of sight.

I found a fir tree to lie under a few feet from the river. The branches hung low, but wide and thick, and the roots were spread just enough to find a nook. I used my backpack for a pillow and found an easy position in spite of the lumps. The night was brisk, and the river cackled just beyond the thicket of blackberry vines overgrowing the banks. I tucked my hands as deep into my jacket pockets as I could. It wasn't exactly warm, but it wasn't miserable, either. With my ankles crossed and my hood pulled up, I figured I could nap for a couple of hours at least.

I thought about making love under the willow tree, to the sound of her river in Eastern Washington. The sounds of the two rivers ran together. I clutched her sun-warmed hips, her breath lapping in short gasps against the moist bank of my ear. Afterward we lay together on a threadbare quilt, listening to the breeze through the willow leaves. The late afternoon heat melted our naked flesh together, and we cooled ourselves in balmy sighs and slightly salty kisses. At the rest stop, though, the wind through the willow leaves was the low growl of a few diesel engines idling, and the subtly murmuring freeway, my own black river. I wrapped myself around the memory of her and tried to sleep.

I dreamt that I followed myself through the little Asian market on the corner of some rainy Seattle street, shuffling like a puppet, the fluorescent lights loosening all the shadows and casting the faces in gory detail. People moved around like empty shells, nobody made eye contact. Every other body was an inconvenience. I bought a twelve pack of beer, some cheap chow mien from the deli, a few votive candles with pictures of saints, and a pack of socks from a box up near the register. I waited in line behind myself, reading an article about Bin Laden's gay lover and waiting for the lady with the credit card problems to find another card. When it was my turn she scanned me through, tossed my things in a plastic bag, and waited as I pulled a wad of crumpled bills from my pocket to pay. I followed myself staggering to the crosswalk, punched the button, looked both ways with one eye clamped shut, and charged the intersection on an empty, but glistening midnight street.

Got up when I got too cold. Couldn't get comfortable anyway. Figured a few hours' rest was good for Rosi. I chugged the Rockstar, took a few puffs off the joint, and smoked a cigarette while I warmed up the engine. The temperature in Oregon would be cooler, and I hoped to get to Portland without too many breaks. Shivering over the bike, I figured a little sun might be nice. Just enough to thaw my fingers. Still had a few hours of dark left.

Traffic was light. I pushed her hard up the pass to enjoy the last few miles out at ninety. The speed limit would change in Oregon, and speeding through the I-5 corridor on an unregistered bike and an out-of-state license didn't seem bright.

The night sky was deep enough to fall into, and the moon cast all the trees in blue. The stars seemed brilliant. To either side, the landscape rolled out crisp and clear. The bugs speckling my visor caught the light from the instrument panel, and I felt like singing again. At least it took my mind off of the cold. *"Stars shining high above you."* As we carved our way up toward the pass, the clouds seemed to gather. *"Night breezes seem to whisper 'I love you.'"*

Rolls of billowing clouds stacked up just beyond the final golden hills.

Storms ahead, Noskivvies muttered.

"Northern Oregon is always cloudy," I said and kept singing, *"When you're all alone and blue as can be,"*

We slowed up the pass.

"Dream a little dream of me."

The clouds became dark towers, and deeper into them, a flat grey wasteland of starless night.

Nope. He said. *Those are definitely storm clouds ahead.*

"Fuck man, can't you be a little optimistic every once in a while?"

That is optimism. We dropped a gear and rolled on some throttle. *Could just be the same boring shit it was the last hundred miles.*

The rain started light at the top of the pass. Streamers ran from the fairing, soaking my shins and thighs. I popped the visor a half-inch to keep it from fogging. It wasn't too bad. I was going to get colder before I got warm, but I was still making good time. The pavement got dark and then turned shimmery, convoys of eighteen-wheelers floated in the river of mist that ran the right lane. As long as I kept to the far left it was bearable. My sneakers were soaked. The rain ran from my view in quivering rivulets. I pushed seventy-five and ran my sleeve over the visor a couple of times. My leather got darker in patches. I've seen storms in the corridor come and go in the time it takes to roll under a bridge. I wasn't worried.

Then it started pouring. Head and taillights glistened and ran. The pavement was black and glossy, the road ahead faded into grey oblivion. Tire ruts filled with water locked me into the center of the lane. I aimed the front tire at anything that didn't look glassy and it got to be like riding a rail. The truckers didn't stop. Even if I'd wanted out, the exits were blocked or hidden by the backwash kicked up. In just a few minutes I was soaked clean through and getting cold fast. Rain stung my knuckles. I would have loved to hear the radio patter between those truckers.

I couldn't let the handlebar go to warm my hands against the engine. I clung to Rosinante praying that she knew the way through the freezing void. Ahead, behind, to both sides, the world was dark, grey, and wet, veiled in the sound of rain against my helmet. I shivered and flexed every muscle to draw blood back into my limbs. My teeth rattled like machine-gun fire and my fingers were dead numb except for the rain that stung like sandpaper across my burnt knuckles. The exit signs ran a green blur above me, illegible. I waited for a blue blur and ducked right into the tunnel of grey *nothing*. Rosi's dials glowed but the rest was a void. Another blue blur ran past my right flank. I eased her toward the shoulder, tracing the line at my feet off the freeway. The truck-wake mist cleared to rain and the rest stop opened up to looming evergreens and a covered area. I hopped off and ran to cover.

Rosinante rested, tendrils of steam rising from her engine case.

I groped in my cigarette pack for the last of the joint and puffed behind a giant map of the Northwest. Bodies seemed to lurk, lost to the anonymity of bad weather. One guy stood talking on a payphone, smoking, and waving his hand around. Another guy stood under the cover near the men's restroom. I was faintly aware of bodies in the parked cars, steamy windows and the sound of hard rain on a car's hood. I walked stiff to the restroom, trying to stretch some of the cold out.

I held my hands under the faucet. The water started. It was cold. I waited, hoping that it might warm up, but it didn't. I splashed it over my face anyway. The fluorescent lights buzzed and cast him cold and drawn. *Yeah, fucker, where's your hot, little princess now, huh?* He glared from the scratched steel rest stop mirror. *How romantic is that rain again?* He laughed. I guess I laughed. It was a sick thing. The man standing at the urinal glanced over and looked away quickly. Noskivvies grinned at me. *You need me, Fuck-o.* I hit the button on the hand dryer, trying my best to ignore him, and turned the chrome nozzle toward my face. The heat made my numb skin tingle.

Where are my pants, and why am I wearing this helmet?

I was near Eugene, sitting outside a motel laundromat waiting for my clothes to dry, stripped down to a pair of happy-face boxers and a T-shirt that used to say "Save the lemmings" until Emira crossed it out and wrote "Kiss Habibi." I was hypothermic. Could barely hold the pen steady and the cold was biting. My hands got dumb out there and I was losing clarity. Not great signs. I sounded like a drunk asking to borrow the dryer. The desk clerk at the Best Western gave me a suspicious sneer. The cleaning ladies in the laundromat just looked worried.

They watched me strip. A couple of middle-aged, matronly types. It must have been exciting. "I don't think I'd want my son riding in the pouring rain."

"I think it's horribly romantic."

"I think it's dangerous." She pushed a wad of sheets into a washing machine. "Stuart has a friend who works for the paramedics…"

"Look at his shirt."

She tried to sneak a peek. I stood upright and showed her my chest. She giggled.

"Sorry. I just think that's awful sweet," the one lady said. "Habibi is your sweetheart, then?"

I nodded.

"What's a lemming?" the other one asked.

"It's a fish, Kathy."

"It is?"

"They wash up on the shore to mate when the tide goes out. You can pick up buckets of them, fry them up like fish sticks."

"No kidding?"

"Brother and his wife went out collecting them last year. Still have bags of them in the freezer."

"How are they?"

"Oh, I don't know. I didn't taste it." She flung an empty laundry bag across the handle of her cart. "You get yourself all warmed up, okay?" She gave me a matronly smile. "Dryer shouldn't take more than forty-five minutes. We'll be right back." She pushed her cart across the parking lot.

When the cleaning ladies came back, they brought me a Styrofoam cup of coffee from the restaurant. It's something warm to wrap my fingers around, at least, shivering so hard I spilled it when I tried to drink. Across the parking lot was a restaurant, looked like it had been there since the mid-seventies, brown-tinted windows and a burnt-looking orange color set into dark brown hardwood. I thought it might be a good place to warm up. I crossed the lot on my tiptoes, like if I could keep my heels dry, that it might somehow prevent the cold that had already crept into my bones.

The dining area had a few customers sitting at the tables, mostly older couples sitting around with coffee and newspapers. The sign at the front said "Please wait to be seated," so I paced and inspected the painting behind the hostess stand. It was a romantic image of several sailors in an old-fashioned dinghy, rowing against the rain and high seas, out toward a big ship farther in the distance.

After a few minutes of waiting, I didn't see a hostess, but a waitress wandered past, doing her best to ignore me. I'm sure they don't get a lot of pantless patrons in for breakfast. The waitress flipped on the neon sign saying that the lounge was open. Good enough. I followed her into the lounge. She hurried ahead of me, probably a bit worried for her safety. Only a matter of time before someone calls the cops or the local mental hospital.

She nestled herself safely behind the bar, and I pulled up a stool. For a few minutes, she continued to ignore me, wiped at the liquor shelves and stacked glasses, peering sideways at my reflection in the big mirror. I eyed myself, folded my hands in front of me and smiled pleasantly. As friendly as I might have looked, I guess I could understand her nervousness. My face was still pale and ghostly, skin chalk white, and blue eyes buried somewhere behind the miles. At last she sighed, turned, and wiping at a clean spot on the bar, confronted the strange, half-naked drunk sitting at the bar.

"Good morning." She faked a smile.

"Good morning." I faked one back.

"Bit of an early riser, aren't you?" She kept wiping at the same spot.

"It's been a long night." I shrugged.

"What can I get for you?"

"Shot of bourbon, please."

She nodded, took a shot glass off of the shelf behind her, and poured out a couple fingers of bourbon. As she was setting the glass on the bar, she read the T-shirt. "What's a lemming?" she asked.

It's something like a suicidal hamster.

"It's a fish," I lied.

"Like save the whales?"

"Yeah, something like that."

"Well, who's Habibi?"

I could hear him laughing. *She's the queen of the suicidal hamsters.*

I bit my lip. "She's my girlfriend," I said.

She faked a smile again. "Well, that's awful sweet."

Yeah, it's giving me a fuckin' cavity just thinking about it. He glared from the mirror behind the bar.

I glared back.

The lounge door opened. An old guy walked in. Dark hair, balding, with a beard. He wore a sheepskin-collared denim jacket, blue jeans, and cowboy boots. He nodded as he shuffled past me. Maybe it's completely normal to find a guy in here in his shorts and a T-shirt.

Now that's what I call a pro. He grinned in the mirror.

I slid the glass to the other side of the bar, hoping for another shot. The bartender was taking care of the old guy at the other end of the bar. He must be a regular, but she didn't give him any shit.

He didn't walk in wearing smiley-face boxers, Sally.

"How do I get rid of you?"

I been asking myself the same thing for a couple months now. Only thing I can figure is you gotta get to the end.

"You die when I reach Habibi?"

Life and death in this place is a fine line. Rosinante is rotting in the garage. You're sitting half-delirious in a basement, surrounded by empty beer cans and the stink of dirty socks. Your sweet, little princess left you months ago because you're a drunk, and the last time you got any sort of love it was your left hand. I mean really, what have you got to lose?

"You're a lying sack of shit."

Yeah, sure, whatever. Let's just finish this, huh? I'm getting sick of this place.

"I can think of a few fantasies I'd rather be having."

Go ahead, man. I dare ya. Make it something good, because frankly, I'm getting sick of this place.

"I want to be with Habibi, lying in the grass beside the river."

Yeah? Well, I just saw the real Habibi just last night, and she told you to leave her the fuck out of your sick, drunken delusions.

"You saw her?"

Saw her and tried to bed her down.

"How is she?"

She looks good enough to eat, as always.

"Did she give us a kiss?"

Yeah, maybe. Doesn't much matter. Can't stop now, fleshbag. The sooner you finish this damn road trip, the sooner we can get out of this basement. Sooner you can get back to the real Habibi, right?

"I'm tired." I shut my eyes.

Bartender, one more. Make it a headstone.

I tucked further into my arms. The bar smelled like finished wood, like old school desks and Simple Green. I let my cheek rest against it. It was cool enough, but it didn't matter much. "It's just a myth."

Aren't we all.

My skin warmed up a little. Even without my clothes I could feel the blood filling me out again. I wanted to sleep. The stool was soft. The bar was soft. Everything was soft. I just wanted to sleep.

If you stop, you die.

I could feel the dark gravity. The light show slowed behind my eyelids. After a few moments, even Noskivvies was still. I sunk into twilight and the bar warmed against my cheek.

There was knock on the bar. It was thunder. I was just about out. At least it got my heart going again. I sat up and looked at the bartender.

"Hey, mumbles." She wiped the bar where my head had lain. I lifted my elbows so she could wipe under them. "I think it's time you finished up," she said.

"Can I just get one more?" I pleaded. "For the ditch."

She poured another, set it on the bar and stood in front of me, waiting for me to finish it.

I downed the shot, paid, and walked out of the lounge. The sun was too bright.

As I crossed the lot, a murder of crows clipped at a bag of fast food. *This is where I leave you, friend.* The crows watched me.

"Can't stand the daylight, huh, Cap'n?"

I'm bored.

As I got close, the crows scattered and took to wing.

The skies cleared up a little bit. Rain eased up. Clothes were almost done. Might as well try it again. If I made it to the Amazons, they'd help. Probably no more than thirty bucks to get home from there.

A few miles on the freeway and the rain started in again. There wasn't much to do for it. I tucked farther over the Rosinante and decided to just ignore the cold.

Living dead

By the time I hit Portland, the doubt, anxiety, and fear were washed clean from my frozen flesh and I was a projectile corpse careening home. I pulled off to the 84 and watched for my exit. I zigzagged through the back streets, shaking so badly that I out-rattled Rosi, her engine hissing at every drip and rivulet that ran down to her engine. On Burnside, I turned right, counted streets until I saw the Blend Café, and parked Rosinante on a side street. I knew that Kristy would never let me leave like this, and I wouldn't be surprised if Lara tried to rush me to a hospital somewhere. When I checked the mirror, my skin was nearly blue and I stared back at myself, glass-eyed and deadly serious.

Thirty dollars' worth of gas and maybe a cup of coffee. That was all I needed. Kristy would help. All I had to do was look serious. Let her know that I meant it. I straightened up, wiped the wet off my face, and tried to shake some warm back into my limbs before I strolled toward the café entrance. Kristy stepped out the front door as I approached. She glanced up at me, set her cigarette to her lips. "Shit, Aaron, you look like hell." She pushed the door open and hollered in. "Lara, Aaron's here!"

I heard Lara call back "Aaron?" and watched her walk through the café toward us, her face changing from joy to abject horror. By the time she reached the door she was charging. "What are you doing to yourself?" She grabbed me and held me up. "Oh my god, you are freezing! You get in here right now."

"I'm f-fine, Lara, fine."

"The hell you are! You're a damn Popsicle." She half-carried, half-dragged me into the coffee shop. "You're crazy. You're soaked to the bone, Aaron. My God!"

Kristy followed us back into the shop. I tried to straighten up and implored with Kristy. "I just w-wanted to stop by and say hello. Maybe see if I c-could borrow thirty dollars for g-gas money."

Kristy looked like she was about to laugh. She shook her head at me.

"I'm s-so close."

"The hell you are," Lara hollered and pushed me toward the heater. "You're close to dead. You reek of gasoline, too. I'm surprised you didn't blow yourself up out there."

"I need to get home."

"You sit yourself down right now."

"I gotta get back to Habibi."

"You gotta get yourself out of those wet clothes and get yourself warm, is what you gotta do."

Kristy poured a big mug of coffee and brought it to me, still smiling and shaking her head at me.

"You and that damn motorcycle," Lara ranted. "I swear you're going to get yourself killed."

"Habibi's waiting for me."

Lara started pulling at my jacket, trying to peel it off of me. "Look at you. You're blue!" She glanced over at a regular customer sitting at a nearby table. "Can you believe this guy?"

Kristy turned up the heat so it blasted down at me.

My skin tingled. "Please, Kristy. I'm almost there."

She snorted laughter.

"What, are you stupid?!" Lara screamed. "You're not going anywhere, buddy. You just drink your coffee."

The hotter Kristy cranked the heat, the worse the tingling in my skin. I felt like I was rolling in a coffin full of nails. Lara kept muttering about me and the damn motorcycle as she returned to the counter to help the next customer. I sipped my coffee with pleading eyes, but Kristy just laughed. "Glad you made it, Aaron."

"I'm so close."

She nodded. "We'll get you warmed up and make sure you get home."

Kristy found a pair of pajama bottoms while Lara made sure that the washer was clear. They waited at the bathroom door while I stripped and handed out wet clothes. Kristy snickered as I handed her my pants. "Damn, boy, your jeans are fuckin' flammable." She held her cigarette away as she passed them to Lara.

"Get that cigarette away from there, punkin," Lara walked them downstairs like they were covered in nitroglycerin. "It's a wonder you didn't blow yourself up."

"I'm almost there."

Kristy snickered again.

"They're not that bad."

She smiled and shook her head. "What am I going to do with you?"

"Loan me thirty bucks?"

"Use my shampoo. It doesn't smell all girly. Scrub good, get all the dirty spots." She flicked her tongue at me and made sexy face as she shut the door. I stood in front of the mirror, a corpse stared back. My face was pale, drawn, and gruesome. I can see why the girls were so worried. I looked dead enough that I probably shouldn't be standing.

I started the water lukewarm and stepped in. Too much heat still made my skin crawl. I don't know how long I stood there, letting the water run over my skull, turning up the hot water a little at a time until it was a steam bath in there. Eventually my blood warmed enough that I was sweating and getting more exhausted by the minute. Maybe the only thing that was keeping me standing was the cold, stiff, and knotted muscles. When I got out, I dried, pulled on the pajamas, and found the girls in the living room watching Oprah. Lara hopped up to make their bed while Kristy packed a bong load for me. She sat next to me on the couch, petted my back, and rested her head on my shoulder. "We thought you'd killed yourself."

"You and everyone else."

"You and that damn motorcycle. It's no wonder."

"I have to call Habibi. She'll be worried."

"That's probably a good idea."

"Just a quick nap, right? Wake me up before it gets too late, would you?"

She snickered. "You're just not giving it up."

"I'm late."

"You're always late. We still love you, though."

I cleared the bong and leaned back on the couch. Kristy handed me the phone. No one answered at Emira's house, so I left a message with the Amazons' phone number. Lara came back into the room. "Alright, mister man, it's time for bed."

"Emira's going to call back. I just need to tell her that I'm okay and that I'll get back on the road again in a few hours."

"You're not going anywhere. You're getting in that bed and getting some sleep."

I looked to Kristy. "Wake me when she calls, please?"

She took the phone from me and pushed my shoulder to get me up off the couch. "Bedtime." Lara took my shoulders to lead me into their room, or just to keep me moving forward.

"Really, Lara, I need to talk to her when she calls."

"I'll tell her that you're here and that you'll be safe with us until you recover."

"Wake me up. She's already pissed." Lara didn't say anything. She just pulled the covers back and pushed me again.

I collapsed on their bed and wriggled into the comforter. If there was ever a time in my life that I was more comfortable, I can't imagine it. Fresh linens and the softest bed I ever laid down on. I was out in a few minutes.

The MOAB at rest

I called every Kawasaki shop in the book, but none of them had a petcock for a 1987 Kawasaki EX500 in stock. They could order one, but it might take weeks and more money than I could reasonably get my hands on. The cycle salvage places didn't know if they had one, and most of them were too long a walk to find out. I was on the curb, contemplating the tank, propped up against a rock to keep from spilling the precious half-gallon I had left. I don't know how long I'd been sitting there. Rosinante took her stand patiently, front wheel turned inquisitively toward me.

Across the street, a screen door opened and a kid stepped out. He had a sword and something else tucked under his arm. He cocked his head at me and shuffled down the front steps sideways. Every time I looked away, he got closer. In a few minutes, he'd crossed the street and taken a seat ten feet down the curb. He played with a stuffed monkey, wrapping its arms around the handle of the sword.

Figuring that I was pretty much screwed on the petcock for a little while, I started pulling the calipers from the front brake.

He took a seat beside me and set his monkey on the concrete in front of us. "My name is Rosco," he said.

I held out my hand. He looked at it and then shook it.

"What's the monkey's name?"

"This is Charlie." He poked at Charlie with his sword. "We're pirates."

"Most pirates have a parrot."

"Charlie flings pooh." Rosco smiled. "He's going to save the world."

"Charlie sounds like one hell of a monkey."

"This isn't the real Charlie. This is just a stuffed animal." He kicked at the monkey with the edge of his sneaker. "The real Charlie is an ape; he has no tail."

"Of course."

"Nobody wants to play with us," he said.

I unscrewed the last bolt and set it in the pile of them. "That's too bad."

Rosco reached out and picked up one of the bolts and looked at it. I resisted the urge to slap it from his hand, like he was going to screw something up just by playing with a bolt.

"What's wrong with your motorcycle?"

"What isn't wrong with it?"

He shrugged. "It looks cool."

"If only that would get me home." I pried at the used pads with my pocket knife, slid the whole setup off the disk and examined them. As I watched, the calipers closed slowly. As much as I pushed, I couldn't seem to open them again. "Fuck," I grumbled.

Rosco looked shocked for a moment and then clapped his hand over his mouth like he was about to laugh. "You said the F word." He smiled.

I pried at them with a knife, but they didn't move much. This probably meant bleeding the brakes, or taking the whole damn setup apart, or something like that. "Stick around; I'll probably say it again."

"My stepdad says that if you cuss, you'll go to hell."

"Yeah? My sister told me that any woman who ever gave a blowjob is going to go to hell, too. Doesn't sound too bad to me."

"Gave a what?"

"Never mind." I crammed the knife between the pads and pried again. The kid scooted a couple of rocks around next to the curb. The knife slipped and cut a gash in my palm. Not a deep one, but deep enough. "Shit," I said.

"You're going to hell." Rosco said plainly.

"As if I weren't already there."

"Hell is full of fire and you burn all the time."

"You know *nothing* of hell, kid."

"My youth pastor told me—"

"Your youth pastor lies." I let the calipers dangle and fished in my pocket for a cigarette, halfway hoping he'd walk away or something.

"Hell is where bad people go," he said, looking a little angry.

"That or government."

"What?"

I've always been of the mind that talking to kids like adults might be the best way to make them adults, but I forget sometimes that not all kids can understand adult concepts like heaven and hell. "Look, Rosco." I took a long drag off my cigarette and blew it up at the clouds. "You go tell your youth pastor that hell hasn't been created yet. It won't happen until the final battle between good and evil, at which time, God will finally open a chasm in the earth and send all the evil people down to burn in hell forever. In the meantime, Satan is walking around the earth, and he could look like anyone: your teacher, your youth pastor, your mom, or your stepdad. The earth itself is hell in the meantime. Auschwitz, Beirut, Hiroshima, Manzanar, Guantanamo-fuckin' Bay, for all I know. Anywhere where one man can have the power to torture and kill another man, that's where hell exists. Humans hurting and killing other humans, and often for very bad, very selfish reasons."

He looked a little shell-shocked. "There's no hell yet?" he asked.

Maybe I was getting through to him. "Not like the church says, at least." I felt bad. Maybe the kid wouldn't eat his vegetables now. "Hell is wherever you make it," I said. I looked at the dangling calipers. "To me, hell is being eternally separated from the thing that you love most."

He leaned back on the curb and kicked his monkey again. He seemed deep in thought. Across the street, a screen door squeaked open and banged shut again. A young cowboy emerged from the house, hat tilted back on his head. He fooled with his red bandana until it was just right and walked down the front stairs. As he neared the bottom step, he adjusted a cap pistol on his hip and took a seat. Rosco glanced across at him.

"That's my brother, Tommy. He talks to crows."

It seemed likely enough. "Do the crows talk back?" I asked.

"Don't be a jerk. Crows can't talk." He leaned over and shielded his mouth with his hand. "But try telling him that."

"Well, why don't you play with him?"

He gave me a funny look. "He's a cowboy," Rosco said.

"So?"

"So pirates can't fight cowboys."

"Why not?"

"Because he doesn't have a sword."

"He has a pistol," I offered.

"So when we fight, he just shoots me every time."

"What if you're bulletproof?" I smiled.

He looked at me like it was the dumbest question he'd ever heard. "It's still not fair. He's older than me."

"So?"

"So he always wins."

I licked the blood from my palm and stared at it, watching the new pool form. It was strangely comforting, as if it was proof that I wasn't in hell after all. How could a living man be wandering around the halls of hell? It's just a metaphor anyway. Can't go getting all caught up in metaphor again.

"I built a castle." He smiled.

I glanced down at the hunk of concrete, balanced on a couple of garden stones.

"That's a nice castle." I smiled back. "But it's missing something."

"What?" he glanced down.

"Maybe a flag?"

He nodded. "Yeah, maybe."

I tore a sheet of paper from my journal and ripped it into a small rectangle. I drew a star on it. Rosco helped me find a small twig to use as a flagpole. Using a few pebbles we propped it up on the top of the concrete chunk.

"You think it needs some little people, too?" I asked, licking my palm.

"It has people."

"Well, where are they?"

He looked down at it and frowned. "They're all inside because there's a duststorm coming."

I looked around at the low-hanging rainclouds. They looked ready to drizzle, but not much more. "Really?" I asked.

"Rip the flesh from your bones," he said, and kicked the castle. The slab bounced a couple of inches, and one of the stones rolled away.

"That's rough," I said.

He shrugged. "It's nature." He walked away.

"Where are you going? What about the castle?'

"I'm going home," he said. He glanced both ways before he crossed the street and strolled across the lawn. Tommy looked up from his seat on the front step. They spoke for a few moments.

Rosco poked at the sidewalk with his stick. Tommy glanced over at me. He tilted his head to the side and then waved like he knew me. I waved back, took a last drag off my cigarette, and ground it out against the curb.

I searched the bathroom for Band-Aids but couldn't find them, so instead I went to the kitchen and dumped salt into the wound. The salt turned red and slushy and then darker red. It burned enough, but it probably didn't do much else. Maybe this sort of thing worked for the Mexicans, but it wasn't doing me much good. I rinsed it, re-salted it, and opened the fridge to see if there was anything in there.

Pickings were getting slim for beer. I pulled an ale out and rifled through the liquor cabinet for some whiskey. As I was pouring my shot, I watched Tommy stroll across the street toward Rosinante. He ran a hand along her seat, squeezed a handle grip, and squatted down next to the front wheel to take a look at the hanging calipers. I poured myself another shot and walked back into the living room. The bong and bag were beside the couch, so I packed a bowl and smoked it watching a few minutes of the news. That just depressed me, so I finally walked back outside. Tommy sat on the curb next to the tank, bent over to look at the paint job without actually touching the tank.

"You must be Tommy," I said.

He squinted up at me and nodded.

"Rosco told me that you can talk to crows." I smiled.

He looked up surprised. "Rosco?"

"Your brother."

He nodded and his face went limp again. "His name is Felipe."

"He told me it was Rosco."

"Rosco was the name of our dog," Tommy said. "He died."

These kids were a regular bundle of happy. "Sorry," I said.

"It's okay." He shrugged. "He was old."

He pulled his cap pistol from the holster and turned it in his hands. After a few turns I saw that he was trying to spin it on his finger. The screen door across the street squeaked and a woman came out. She glanced up and down the street, saw us on the curb and called to Tommy. He stood, put his gun back in his holster, and turned to me. "That's my mom. I gotta go."

I waved at her, but she didn't wave back. I guess these days parents got to suspect I'm a molester or something. "See ya, Tommy," I said.

He waved as he walked away. When he got up the front steps, she cuffed him upside the head, hard enough to knock his hat off. She grabbed his arm, shuffled him in through the front door, and shot an angry glare at me. I imagine I must be a very bad man to her. I wonder what Felipe told her. There's no hell yet? Hell is here on Earth? The youth pastor might be Satan? Any woman who ever gave a blowjob is going to hell? I hope it was a good one. Maybe he just said fuck or something.

I pulled another cigarette from my shirt pocket. The pack was dwindling. I had maybe five or six left. I flicked a match and lit it, focusing on the brake calipers hanging from the front fork. If C clamps didn't fix it, *nothing* would. Without them, there wasn't much way to slide the burnt-out pads back onto the disk. I suppose I'd been running with shitty brakes most of the way, but at least there was something. I couldn't very well go barreling home with the front brake calipers dangling the whole ride.

As I resolved myself to walking the ten blocks to a hardware store, I happened to glance over to where the boys had been sitting. There, pretty as you please, sat a new castle. Tommy had rebuilt it while I was inside getting a beer. The new castle was set sturdily atop a few extra rocks and pine cones, and the flag flew proudly from the top of the asphalt stronghold. Beside the flag, a red plastic gunman stood, palms poised at his pistols, ready for the clock to strike high noon.

Kristy walked up and stood behind me, looking over the leaking tank and the brake cables hanging loose. For just a moment, she looked strangely like her father. "How's it going?" She pulled a cigarette from her pack and placed it to her lips. "You think it's safe to smoke?" She raised her eyebrows at Rosi and flashed her lighter.

I nodded and scooted back on the sidewalk, patting the spot beside me. "Takes an open flame to set the MOAB off."

She lit her smoke before she stepped forward. She handed me a package of J-B Weld. "My father swears by this shit," she said. "Found some in my tool box."

I read the package. There were testimonials from farmers. If it could fix a tractor, it should be able to fix a leaky petcock. "How was work?" I asked.

She took a seat, carefully placing her ass on the concrete. "Good. Busy early. We made decent numbers."

"Nice."

She nodded. "Yeah, small talk." She smiled stony and latched her eyes on me.

"Just asking," I said.

She nodded and tapped her smoke on the edge of the curb. "Honestly, we're a little worried about you, Aaron."

I laughed lightly. "I always make it."

"You could have died out there. I mean, if the rain didn't get you, there was a good chance you'd set yourself on fire."

"But I didn't."

"That's not the point."

"Isn't it?" I pulled a cigarette out of my shirt pocket and lit it. "I mean, I've covered almost twelve-hundred miles so far, riding a busted-ass motorcycle on one cylinder, half-delirious and the other half high on love, chain smoking over a gas leak." I took a drag and blew a cloud from my grin. "And you know, the fucked-up part is, in spite of my stupid, self-destructive behavior, I'm still not dead yet."

She took a puff from her cigarette and nodded. It was enough for me to continue.

"Didn't you ever see yourself as somebody else? Somebody better than all of this? I mean, maybe I read too much, but I always wanted to be some sort of hero, somebody bigger and faster and stronger and smarter and everything that I wasn't."

"But you're still just a boy, Aaron."

"Yeah." I smiled. "I know." I rolled the cherry of my cigarette against the curb, preening the ashes. "And life gets messy, and I get tired and beaten and broken, just like everybody else." I smiled at her.

She tried to smile back.

For two people who have no sexual attraction, the eye contact can get a little too honest sometimes. There is an intimate place, where people are just people, and honesty is as unavoidable as death. I didn't have to tell her that I was going to do it, no matter what. I didn't have to tell her that whether she liked it or not, I was getting back on that motorcycle. I still had a half-tank, and short of death, *nothing* could stop me. I smiled and butted my forehead against her shoulder. "Maybe I'm just a boy, a frail, mortal thing, and one day I'll die, just like everybody else." I took a drag and inspected the burning ember at the tip. "Maybe I'm already a dead man." I exhaled another cloud. "But that fucker Noskivvies, He lives." I grinned. "He lives like he knows there's *nothing* else. And so long as he lives, he'll drag my puppet corpse along with him like an anchor."

Our eyes pleaded with each other; plied at a border skirmish.

"C'mon, Kristy. I've come too far to stop now. If I quit here, I'm just another guy. I'm a fucking fleshbag on a burnt-out old nag. I'm an alcoholic bum crashing on your couch because it's easier than the street. I'm still just a few miles away from immortality." I took a drag and frowned. "If I quit now, I'm just human."

"And what's wrong with being human?"

"*Nothing*, I guess, unless you can think of something better."

"And this girl is worth dying for?"

"It was always the sea I was in love with. The mermaid was just an excuse."

"Then if you were always doing it for the sea, maybe you were always doing it for you."

"Maybe."

"Then if you quit now, you really haven't lost anything, have you?"

I never really thought of it like that. I mean, I guess I always knew she was just a figurehead, a siren of some sort, but who was it really that was singing? Was it the Dulcinea who I created, or my own subconscious? Was Galatea made entirely by my hand, or was there an inspiration? The very act of creation is so intimate and indescribable that even I can't tell the difference between what I made and what made me. The dream girl was a figure. A template. A face, distant and indistinct. She was a default muse, the form my mind wandered to when there was *nothing* left to choose, the form my hands made when I left them to wander. "Yeah, maybe. But what if..?"

She smiled. "What are we going to do with you, Aaron?"

"Give me thirty bucks so I can get back to Habibi?" I laid my head on her shoulder.

"Ah," She tugged my blond streak and petted my head. "You fix that gas leak, and we'll talk." She was about to put her cigarette out against the curb, but looked up at the petcock and the tank. She smiled and standing up, ruffled my hair again.

The J-B Weld came in two sticks. A light one, and a dark one, like chemical blocks of yin and yang. I unwrapped them like chocolate bars, just enough to get a decent chunk out of either side, cutting it against the concrete. It had been years since I played with anything malleable, but kneading it between my palms, the two sides rolled together, twisted together, and crushed back into a swirling ball. With each pass of my palms the swirls of epoxy and catalyst blent up to a single pale grey wad, leaving their traces in my palms, asphalt patches in the fissures of my life line and fingerprints. When it was a decent grey wad, and getting warm, I puttied the hell out of the petcock and left it on the curb to cure.

Cowboy in the kingdom of the Amazons

A bottle of Ronsonol lighter fluid is a one-night-stand liquor-store fix. It is fire quick and sloppy, and despite the fact that everybody is protected, it still feels dirty somehow. It's not the long, slow, methodical lovemaking of a good lamp-oil-soaked wick just before sunrise. It's not the hard, eager burn of a fresh white-gas-heavy mix while the DJ is still spinning and the bass is just opening up a place to lay a backbeat. No, a single bottle of lighter fluid is *nothing* compared to these. It is a single-serving bottle of quick-and-easy pyromance. This is a rogue burn, in somebody's backyard, and there is always a chance that a neighbor might call the cops.

I stood out on the back patio, with the Amazons and a few of their friends looking on, watching me squeeze the contents of a one night stand all over my wicks, soaking them as best I could, and wondering how fast it was evaporating. Kristy came down off of the porch with her lighter. "Good thing we washed the gas off those jeans," she said.

"You know, I had hoped to die in a fiery ball of flames." I hung the rope around my neck and pulled on my gloves.

"Not yet, Aaron." She took my cigarette from my lips and tossed it on the ground behind her. "You ready?"

I nodded.

She flicked her lighter under my wicks, and the fire jumped. "I have a wet towel," she said, but it was crumpled on the corner of the porch.

I smiled. "Thanks."

She stepped back slowly. I think she likes the sound of fire as much as I do, and when it first dropped into a swing, she grinned, backing out of the flickering light. The wicks pendulumed three or four times, and swung out into their opening throes, a single hot ball of light spiraling into my personal orbit.

With the Amazons, I didn't really feel the meditation the same way. It wasn't sinking into my burn sphere or getting lost in the dance, but more a kinetic candlelit conversation. It was an intimate burn, set on a cobbled brick patio with pine trees for pillars all around. A court jester routine for the royal family. They heckled and chuckled amongst themselves. I smiled and laughed with them, warned the first-timers that I'm a little drunk, and they may want to be ready to dial 911. Lara assured them that I've been drunker than this and still put on a good show.

But I couldn't keep it open, fluttering out there, too far, too much space between. The spin was too hard. I had to pull it in, soft kiss every moment, and drag the beauty out of the ephemeral, crackling bright for that one last, long distance dance. I switched back, folded the rope to a single orbit, wrapped it around my legs to draw in the slack, split it tight, and wrapped up the excess rope in my fists. As the fire came in, it burned hotter, in tiny circles between my fists. The one, chasing the other, forever and ever, amen. Even closed in, it was hard to keep the flames bright.

As the wicks started to sputter, I released loops, letting the rope stretch itself out, slowly, slowly, until it was again the single orbital, in a low arc around my legs. With a flourish, I spun, whipped it up quick around my head like a wide halo, and spun it out to a dark, smoking mass. The Amazons clapped and whistled, and the wicks smoked out, hanging together in front of me.

Proof of *nothing*

I woke up in my old room, upstairs. I opened my eyes to a water glass on the nightstand, a feminine Chapstick lip print on the edge. Beside it lay a few hairpins. I lay there for a while, wondering if they were there when I passed out, or if they appeared overnight.

The girls tell me that it's my room, but I never actually lived there. It was mostly an office, with an attached spare bedroom. It had a desk, filing cabinet, some nondescript furniture in every corner. A single bed that was comfortable enough. If anyone else ever stayed there, I never saw evidence. I used it whenever I passed through. But it was my room. The water glass and hairpins made no sense. I sat up, finally, and pulled on my jeans.

Kristy left forty dollars and a couple of nugs on the coffee table next to the bong. In the kitchen, Lara had loaded the coffee maker with Stumptown grounds, left a single mug next to it, and a Post-It note that said: "Turn me on!"

I watched some crappy TV while I waited for coffee to brew, and smoked half of what Kristy left me. I turned on the news channel, but all they were talking about was politicians and Wall Street. There was *nothing* more about the ongoing wars. I drank a cup of coffee, smoking my morning cigarette inside, just because I could, and walking around in my jeans, which, after a few good road washes, were finally beginning to fit just right.

By the time I got out to the curb, it was almost eleven. I lit a cigarette and inspected the J-B Weld patch job on the petcock. That shit was solid as stone. On the curb, next to the screws that held the petcock in place, someone had taken the last of the pliable J-B Weld, rolled it out into a thin chord, and made it into the shape of a heart. Somehow, it brought me back to the hairpins. Had Habibi been here? As I slept, perhaps? Had she slept with me? Had I slept alone? I found evidence of her everywhere, but still no body. *Nothing*. So much *nothing*.

I squatted down next to the bike and slid the tank across the asphalt beside me. Setting the hardened putty heart aside, I set about screwing the petcock back onto the tank, reattaching the fuel lines, and replacing the tank. I replaced the front brakes with the pads I sent ahead. While checking through the repairs, I found a pink plastic ribbon tied to the throttle-side handlebar.

I kicked at the saddle bags a couple of times, but they still seemed like too much luggage. I put on my boots, and grabbed a couple pairs of socks, just in case I had to lose the pair I had, but the rest of it had become useless to me.

I zipped up my jacket, pulled on my helmet and gloves. Armored from head to toe in brown leather and blue denim, I straddled Rosinante. When I pushed the button, she started right up.

Blue skies and tailwinds

I took it easy through the neighborhoods, getting a feel for Rosinante. I tapped her front brakes at the stoplights, testing the new pads, and checked the petcock at every stop, to make sure that it hadn't started leaking again. We moved easily towards the freeway, taking random turns, watching for the on ramp signs, navigating by intuition. Fact is, I was profoundly stoned as well, but after twelve-hundred miles I just felt more comfortable driving.

The few days' rest had put me back together. The muscles in my shoulders and arms were flesh again, but tighter for the travels, as if I'd burned off the soft padding of my recent domesticity. I felt solid. Rosinante herself seemed stronger, like a set of brake pads and a wad of plumber's epoxy were all that she needed in the first place. Dropping onto the freeway she sounded better, and I pushed her hard up into her power band, the tachometer needle bouncing as I hopped through gears.

My curbside conversation with Kristy still rattled around in my head like a ball bearing at the bottom of an empty can of flat black spray paint. I said it before I thought it. It was always the sea I was in love with, the mermaid was just an excuse. It didn't really matter what happened next. The deed was as good as done. But then what?

For all my talk over the months before, I hadn't really planned to make it all the way to Portland, let alone bringing Rosinante up to speed on the final hundred-mile stretch leading up to Habibi's house. I tried to envision myself pulling into the driveway in eastern Washington, road hardened and dressed in my armor, hoping that she might see me as the man she had once fallen in love with.

There was a chance at least, that's all I needed, just a chance. Once she saw me, and we were close again, she would have to love me again. After all, if I had made it all the way from

Southern California on a rusted out nag, she would have to see that anything was possible. It was proof of something where *nothing* seemed to exist.

The sky was an impossible blue, a fleck of moon hanging off to one side like a flaw in its crystal clarity. As the buildings and side streets became fewer and further between, trees and underbrush replaced them, cliffs rising up to one side, and the freeway edged up against the Columbia River itself. From there it would be miles and miles of desert highway, and following various rivers until I was finally home.

With a hundred miles left, I got to feeling fairly confident. There was no way for her to ignore me when I was knocking down her front door. On an open stretch, with *nothing* left to lose, I opened the throttle little by little until it got to be less like driving than low altitude flying. “Almost home, Rosinante.” But my voice was lost to the screaming exhaust pipe, and the wind tearing me to pieces.

Happily ever after, and all that crap

At 117 miles per hour, there was a loud pop from the left side of the bike. Something flashed and the engine cut out. She jerked and I fell forward against the tank. I hit the clutch, and Rosinante was a free-rolling missile. Dead weight careening above the asphalt. Her left flank was hot and when I glanced down, I felt the nearly invisible flicker of flames on her engine block.

Somebody told me once that it would be bad to put out an engine fire with water. And worse than putting out an engine fire with water, it would be bad to put it out with a water bottle full of lamp oil that only looked like water. I can't imagine what most people would do if they skidded to the side of the road on a burning motorbike.

I got to the side of the highway, ripped my fire safety rag out of my gear bag, and patted out the flames, flickering on the old oil and grease on Rosinante's engine. I'm trained for this. I am the lucky one. The sparkplug hung limp from its cable, the gap charred to shit, and smoky. I tried screwing the plug back into the engine, but she still wouldn't fire on the second cylinder; at least not enough to ride her. I lay on a grass embankment, my helmet for a pillow, my armor for a bed. I was smoking my fourth cigarette. I had three left. The sun was high and hot. I scraped at the charred end of the sparkplug with my thumbnail, willing it to grow a new gap.

Laying by the side of a desert highway might seem romantic and all, but the thought occurred to me that there was no rescue team coming, and this time, I might actually be on my own. No phone, no roadside assistance package on my nonexistent insurance, and still a good hundred miles from a woman who might not want to see me. Maybe the way would write itself, but in a case like this, the way might need a bit of a hand.

I stood up, shook the grass off my jacket and picked up my helmet. I unstrapped the backpack, tied my jacket to it, and started walking.

The Jake Brakes growled hard behind me as it slowed, red lights dim. The semi eased over to the shoulder, cutting me off, kicking up a cloud of dust.

As I walked past the cab, the passenger door opened and a tan-colored miniature poodle yapped from the passenger seat down to me. He looked like a little, brown lamb. "Peanut!" the driver yelled. The poodle turned around, shook its tail and leapt to the driver's lap. The driver leaned over to get a look at me. He was mid-thirties, maybe, a crumpled, sage-colored fisherman's cap pulled down over his sunglasses, a full beard with a smirk. "That your bike back there?"

I nodded, raised the helmet to show him, making sure he couldn't see the Arabic writing, just in case.

"Bad idea to leave it on the shoulder," he said. "Somebody might hit it."

"It's dead anyway," I said.

"Outta gas?"

"Blew a sparkplug out the engine and the thing caught fire."

"Just ain't yer day, is it?" He laughed. "Hop in." The poodle started yapping again. "Damnit, Nutbiter, shutup."

"I can walk." The last thing I needed was to hop in the cab with another patriot redneck trucker.

"I'm sure, kid, but you're a good five miles from the next stop, and another twenty or so from a parts store."

I glanced down the highway, judging distances, the sun creeping across the sky.

"Just get in. We don't bite." He scratched the dog's butt and tucked him into his lap. "At least he don't unless you're running, then he goes straight for the sack, you know?" He pulled the stacks of papers from the passenger seat, tossing them over his shoulder into the sleeper.

I climbed up into the cab and pulled the door shut.

"Name's Scott, and this is Peanut." He patted the dog's head. Peanut had an afro and a puff of chest hair, and kept looking up to Scott with his tongue hanging out. "Go ahead, sniff him."

I held out my knuckles for the dog to sniff. He checked me and glanced back at Scott. "He's gay," he said. "I think it's because my sister got his nuts cut off." The dog stood and leaned against his chest, licking at his lips. "Yeah, yeah." He sat the dog down again.

He didn't look much like a redneck. He was in board shorts, an old T-shirt, and stomped the peddles bare foot. When he turned back to the highway he was smirking. As he eased it back out into the first lane, the radio squawked and crackled. He leaned forward, turned it down and leaned back again. "Lost a plug and caught fire, huh?"

"Yeah."

"Sucks." He chuckled.

"Yeah."

"Thing's a turdboiler." He chuckled again.

I glanced out the window and watched him creep his rig back up to cruising speed. His seat was all the way forward, but he was leaned back. He jerked the stick back and forth, rattling it to make sure it engaged. Peanut watched me, lying across Scott's lap with his tongue hanging out of his mouth.

"So the dog only bites if I'm running?" I asked.

"In the nuts," he said, hunched forward to shift, and glanced out the side view mirror.

"Fair enough," I said.

He laughed. "Long ride, huh?"

"Not done yet," I said and looked down the highway.

He nodded, chuckled again, checked the mirrors, yanked it down to fourth, and accelerated through. "Rugged independent and all, right?"

"Sure." I stared down the highway.

"I ain't here to get up in your business. I just figured you might need a hand."

"Thanks, man."

He popped through a couple more gears. The transmission seemed infinite.

"So what are you hauling?"

"You right now. Trailer's empty. I'm deadheading it to Kennewick."

"What are you picking up?"

"Human bodies, toxic waste maybe, fuck if I know."

"You haul toxic waste?"

"How come nobody ever asks about the human bodies?"

"I assume you're joking about bodies."

"I don't know. Don't care, either." He scratched Peanut's head. "I just drive." He stared down the freeway. He smiled and nodded like he'd thought something he liked. "Yes sir," he said. The Jake Brake growled a little hard between gears. We sped up a bit. I barely felt it.

"Must be a great job," I said. "Just drive."

He nodded, wagged his head from side to side, and shrugged. "It's okay," he said. "Hours get long after a while. We get quiet." He scratched Peanut's head again.

I nodded.

We rode on in silence. After a few moments, the rig hummed again.

"What's that?" I asked.

"Compressor," he said.

I nodded like I knew what his rig needed a compressor for. I guess I expected the leviathan to make more noise. The cab towered over traffic. I watched the fisheye lens for cars. They were silent and distorted. A motorcycle must be less than the blink of an eye. I tried to imagine myself out there, sailing invisible past his flank. He let the Jake Brake growl and shifted again. Peanut licked his shifting arm a few times. Scott glanced down at my jacket. "You starting a bug collection?"

I checked the jacket, there was a decent mess going on the front of it, black-and-yellow splotches, a collection of abandoned wings glued to the leather by abandoned guts. I started brushing them off unconsciously, then realized that I was brushing bug guts all over the floor of his cab. I glanced up at him. He chuckled again.

"Don't worry about it." He scratched the dog's head. "Peanut's done worse in here."

"Sorry."

"Forget it."

We rode in silence for a few more minutes. "That's a fancy paint job on that helmet," he said.

I checked the paint. There were a good number of bug splats on it too. I rolled it away from him. "Yeah."

"You do it yourself?"

I nodded.

"What's it say?"

"Habibi," I said. "It's Arabic. It means 'my lover.'"

He nodded, smiled, and nodded again. "I like that."

I was actually expecting him to stomp the brakes and pull the rig to the side of the road, but he didn't. "She must be somethin' else, got you out here on the side of the road, middle of nowhere."

I nodded. "Yeah; I guess she must be."

He smiled back. "You think you can fix that thing?"

I shrugged. "It caught fire."

"Anything burn up?"

"Some oil."

"Should be fine. How's that plug?"

I pulled it out of my pocket and passed it over to him. He leaned forward over the wheel, eyeing the gap. "Thing's burnt to shit. What you been doin' to that bike?"

"Riding."

"How far?"

I checked over my shoulder, looking out of the cab, down at the ditch beside the freeway, as if the mileage were written somewhere in the gravel there. "About twelve hundred miles, I guess."

He shook his head. "She must be something special." He passed back the plug. "Still got threads?"

"Threads?"

"In the engine case."

"Yeah," the part that the plug screws back into. "Yeah, it's still got threads."

"How far you got left to go?"

I glanced down the freeway, to where it disappeared over the horizon. "About a hundred miles, I guess."

He nodded, smiled, and scratched Peanut's head. "What do you think, Nutbiter?" The dog looked up at him, curly hair hanging down over his eyes. "Yeah; I think so, too." He didn't say anything else for a couple of miles. A mile before the exit he downshifted and the truck growled. He pulled off the freeway, around a corner, and down a backroad. At one of the lights, he sat forward, eyed the mirror on my side, and took a wide turn onto another backstreet. A few blocks in, he ground his rig down to a stop.

"There's a parts store tucked back into the mall there. Go get 'em, kid."

I collected my gear, opened the cab door, and started stepping down.

"You don't find a ride right away, stick to the westbound lanes for a few miles. I'll be coming back this way in a few hours. I'll get you back to that scooter."

"That's alright. I'll be fine."

He nodded, smirked, and sweeping his fishing cap off his head, scratched his Mohawk. "Yeah, I'm sure. But just in case, I wouldn't mind seeing just what a happily ever after looks like." He nodded.

"Thanks, man."

He smiled, "Nah, thank you."

The last rest stop

A couple sat a few stools down. The guy was shaggy, buzz cut growing out, a week's beard, and a raggedy, sleeveless black T-shirt. He nursed a pint glass of something that looked like juice, but he winced every time he took a drink. He kept his other arm wrapped around the girl's shoulder. She looked Latina, big brown eyes and curly black hair pulled back into a pony tail. She leaned into him, kissing his neck. He smiled and held his head high so that she could kiss up under his chin. She was smiling when she glanced at me, and there was something catlike about her eyes, watching me. She kissed up to his ear and must have said something, because he laughed. He glanced over at me, looked me over, and shrugged. "Nah, baby," he said. "*No pienso.*" She whispered something else and he laughed. "*Possivlemente.*" He looked at me out of the corner of his eye and snorted. She turned his face to hers, kissed him hard, and whispered something into his lips. "Okay, baby." As she got up to walk away, he tried to pinch her butt and she frowned at him playfully. I looked away, embarrassed, trying to imagine what she said. I didn't want to imagine Habibi checking out another guy while she was kissing me.

We both watched her walk away. He caught me looking and scowled. He licked his lips, shook his head, and picked up his pint glass again. When the waitress walked by he said something to her. She nodded and came back with an ashtray a few moments later. He pulled a pack of cigarettes from his pocket, shook one out, and just before he lit it, glanced over at me again. "You don't mind if I smoke, do you?"

I shook my head. "I forgot you can still smoke in restaurants here."

"Damn civilized," he said. He blew the smoke up, waved it away, and picked up his pint glass again. "Whatcha writing?" he asked.

I glanced down at the few lines in my notebook and shrugged. “Just notes.”

“Journal or something?”

I nodded. “Or something.”

He nodded again.

The waitress came around with a coffee pot and refilled my mug. I wrapped my fingers around it and pulled it closer.

“You want another?” she asked him.

He glanced over his shoulder to the restroom. “Yeah, what the hell.” He slurped down the rest of his drink and slid it across the counter to her.

“Where you headed?” he asked, nodding toward my helmet.

“Eastern Washington.” I said.

“Engine problems?”

I glanced at my keys, helmet, and knapsack. “How’d you know?”

“I saw you playing with the sparkplug.”

“Blew it out the side of the engine,” I said.

“Damn.”

“Mind if I bum a smoke?”

“Nah.” He slid the pack and chrome Zippo down the counter.

I took a smoke, lit it, and slid the pack back down to him. “Damn civilized.” I nodded.

He nodded back. “Yup.” He took a long pull off his cocktail and winced again.

The girl walked up behind him and wrapped her arms around his neck. “Another?”

“No scurvy, baby.”

I snorted a laugh. He glanced down at me. “So what brings you guys out here?” I asked.

“Travelling. Got to show the girl my home. Figured we’d take the long route.”

“Where you from?”

“Oaxaca.” He smiled.

“*Mentiroso*.” She pushed his shoulder.

“Around,” he said.

She frowned at him and smiled apologetically at me. She whispered something to him again.

“No way, baby.” He shook his head.

"I think so."

He wrinkled his nose and glared. "*Que, otro sancho*?"

She scowled, then pouted. "Baybee." She smoothed his hair back. "That's no funny. *Te amo*, baby."

"*Y yo a ti mas*," he growled, waggled his eyebrows, and gave her a carnal grin.

"Baby!" She smiled, leaned back, and slapped his shoulder.

"*Quieres ayudar?*"

"*Si quieres.*"

"Alright." He leaned back, checked the last of his drink, slurped it down, and rubbed his face. He sighed hard and turned toward me, one eye clamped shut. "Wanna ride?"

"I can walk."

"Yup." He nodded, looked back to his drink, sighed again, and bowed his head. "Yeah, what the hell," he said and kicked back from the bar without looking up. "Grab yer shit; let's get the fuck out of here."

He reached for the check, read it, and pulled a crumpled wad of bills out of his pocket.

"Baby," she said.

"No baby, I got it."

He slapped a few bills down, turned away from me. Whatever he said to her, she liked it. She threw her arms around his neck and kissed him like it was a wedding proposal. When she started digging her claws in, I turned away. "You ready?" he asked.

"I have to pay."

"I got it." He waved at the waitress, pointed at me and at the wad of bills. "Let's do this shit."

I collected my helmet and bag and dug into my pocket for a tip.

"I got it, man; don't sweat it." He wrapped his arm around his girl's neck and tried to bite her head. She pushed her sunglasses up and clawed his neck again. Maybe walking wasn't such a bad idea.

I followed them across the parking lot to a little blue-silver Nissan sedan. He unlocked the passenger door, opened it for her, and held it as she got in. "*Estas Bien?*" He asked. "*Si,*" she said. He shut the door and walked around the front of the car. These guys were unreal. She unlocked the doors and we climbed in.

He turned the key, leaned across to the passenger side, and kissed her cheek as she looked through her purse. "*Te amo,* baby," she said, without looking at him. The radio started up playing Mexican music.

"You like reggaeton?" he asked.

"Is that a band?"

"East or west?" he asked.

"Uh, west."

"Perfect." He eased out of the parking lot and stopped at the light. "It's a type of music," he said.

"Sure, I guess. I like everything."

She sat in the front seat pushing through buttons on her cellphone.

"*No sirve?*" he asked.

She shook her head and stuffed her phone back in her purse.

"I think we got to get closer to some sort of a city."

"I think so," she said.

He sat forward in his seat and checked the rearview like there might be traffic coming. "Hang on." The engine whirred as he picked up speed.

"So where are you going?" she asked, and turned a little in her seat.

"Eastern Washington," I said.

"Yes, but why?"

"To see my girl."

"On a motorcycle?"

"Yeah."

"I think she must miss you," she said.

"I hope so."

"You do not know?"

I watched the river pass outside, thought about the last few miles between us. "She doesn't answer my calls right now."

"That is very sad," she said. "If my baby were far away, I think I would miss him very much." She leaned toward him and petted his head.

"Baby," he said, and rested the back of his fingers against her lips. She kissed his knuckles.

"I think she must miss you," she said.

"Yeah; I hope so."

"Is that it?" He pointed at Rosinante as we careened around a soft curve.

"Yeah, that's it," I said.

He pulled on his seatbelt.

"Baby?" She checked her seatbelt and scooted into her seat.

He pulled her hand up to his and kissed her knuckles. "Hang on, baby." He popped it into fourth. "Here we go." He stomped the brake and jerked around in the seat, checking all the mirrors and blind spots. She grabbed the handle and sunk into her seat. "Baybeee," she warned.

"No cop, no stop." He checked. At a gravel stretch he steered into the median, cranked the wheel hard left and four-wheel drifted into the dip.

"Baybeeeee!" She hung tight to the handle and bounced around in the seat. "What are you doing?"

"I don't know." He laughed. "I've never done this before. He yanked it into third, slid up the other side of the median, spinning tires and bounced back onto the freeway in a clamor of gravel hitting wheel wells and the little Nissan engine whizzing in vain.

"You are crazy." She leaned back against the door and pouted.

He pushed it into fourth, glanced over his shoulder, veered across to the first lane, and downshifted through third and second as he rolled up behind Rosinante. "Fuck yeah," he said, and stomped the brakes in a cloud of dust.

"Baby!" She slapped his shoulder.

"*Que?* We made it, didn't we?"

"Be nice to my car."

"Ah baby, I didn't wreck it." He flicked on the hazards and jerked on the emergency brake. "Last stop, housewares, linens, and busted-ass motorbikes."

"Thanks for the ride," I said.

"No problem," he said, but I'm not sure he knew I was there. He watched her stretch in the passenger seat. When she stopped and turned to him, he leaned over and buried his face in her neck.

She giggled and pushed his face away, rubbing the stubble along one cheek. "*Me dan cosquillas,* baby."

"*Si bebe, quieres cosquillas?*" he pushed his way over into the passenger seat and started tickling her. She wriggled and giggled and writhed.

"No baby!" She clawed his neck and giggled some more.

Yeah, they didn't even know I was there. I checked the traffic before I opened the door and left the two of them wrestling in the front seat. A semi rumbled past and left me in the wake, the little Nissan rocking. When I knelt down to screw the sparkplug in, I checked them again. They were kissing, his feet hanging out of the driver's side door. For all I could tell, they might be going at it in there.

I didn't understand what she saw in him; she was gorgeous and well put together, where he was shaggy and ragged and looked like he might have just stepped out of a bad Quentin Tarantino flick. When I looked back, he was pushing himself out the driver's side window, legs hanging out looking for ground, and half of his body still stuffed in the car. She laughed in the passenger seat and swatted at him.

A few moments later, he strolled up next to me.

"You guys don't have to wait for me." I told him.

"Yeah, but it's a long walk to a bus stop if that thing doesn't start again."

"It'll start, it has to."

"Right, well, just in case." He pulled his cigarettes from his back pocket. "Besides, she gets cell service here. Can't leave until she finishes her phone call."

I hand cranked the sparkplug in as far as I could.

"Smoke?" he offered me a cigarette.

"Sure."

"That thing isn't going to catch on fire again, is it?"

"I don't think so."

He paced up to the white line and stretched like he was about to dive into the asphalt.

"How long have you guys been going out?" I asked.

He massaged his forehead and squinted down the highway to where she sat in the passenger seat. "Shoot, almost two years." He made a kissy face at her.

"Still in love?"

He laughed. "Oh, I'm good and screwed." He took a drag off his smoke, inspected the front of the bike, and picked at one of the zip ties holding the windshield on. "Keeps up like this, I think I might try to marry her."

"She's gorgeous," I said.

He nodded, gave me a cold look, and glanced back at her. "Fuckin' smart, too, but of course no one ever says that."

I laughed. As I was trying to set the cable back onto the end of the plug, he stood behind me. "Might want to bolt that plug in a little better than that, or you'll probably blow it out again."

"No tools," I said.

"Hmm." He sauntered back toward the car and leaned in the passenger-side window. She kissed him.

He popped the trunk and rifled through the back, pulling out a sleeping bag and throwing it up on the roof. She put her feet up on the dashboard and played with her toes. He came back with a little duffle bag of tools. "Don't think this is going to help much, but just in case." He dropped the bag next to me and squatted next to the back tire. I dug into the bag, looking for a tool I didn't figure would be there, but when I found the ratchet, it had the head I needed already on it. I tested it on the plug. "Fuck me; it's a perfect fit."

"Aren't you the lucky one?"

I cranked the plug down. "You guys are really affectionate," I said.

"Yeah, we make people sick."

"I wasn't saying that." I put the tools back in the bag.

"You don't have to."

"You guys are like high-school kids."

"Yeah, it used to bug me too. I mean, pissed off a few bartenders and wore out a few single friends, but then I kind of figured, what the hell? The world is full of people who want to hate. Seems like there should be room for a couple that want to be in love."

"There's probably a room somewhere," I said.

He chuckled. "There have been a few rooms."

"It's a good philosophy, at least."

"Man on a motorcycle riding back to his girl, I figure you must get it."

"Not as much as I used to." I smiled. "Not out here, at least." I passed him the tool bag. "Wish I could thank you somehow."

"Don't worry about it."

"You, uh, smoke pot?"

He glanced back at the car. "The girl doesn't, but I guess I could smoke hers."

I pulled one of the joints out of my pocket and offered it to him.

"Oh no," he laughed. "You gotta light that shit. No way I'm gettin' popped for your fuckin' joint, man."

"Fair enough." We hunkered down with our backs to the bike and freeway. I lit the joint, took a few puffs, and handed it off to him. "If that's all it takes."

He took a long draw from it, lurched like he was about to cough, and grinned. "Ah yeah." He grunted and tried to pass it back.

"Take your time, man."

He nodded, took another puff and glanced over at the car.

"She get upset when you smoke?"

He shrugged. "I can drink as much as I want and all, but Mexicans get weird about pot."

"That's cause they grow shitty pot down there."

"Yeah." I offered him the joint, but he shook his head. "Probably better hit the road soon," he said.

"Yeah."

He stood and picked up the tool bag. "You think you'll be alright from here?"

I plugged the cable in again, pushed the key into the ignition, and pushed the button. Rosi turned over. "Sounds good." I gunned the throttle a couple of times and she sounded decent. "Yeah, think I might make it this time."

His girlfriend got out of the car and walked toward us. She stretched and smiled. "You fixed it?" she asked.

"Yup."

"Do you think you will be okay?"

"Oh yeah."

She wrapped her arms around his neck and kissed his cheek.

"Ready to go, baby?" he asked.

She whispered something in his ear.

"Again?"

"Si, baby."

"You think all gringos look alike," he said and kissed her.

"I'm serious," she said. She kissed him again and frowned at him. "You smoked pot?"

"Anyway," he said, "we gotta get back on the road."

"Baby?" she asked.

"Yeah, I took a few hits."

"Then I will drive."

"Fine."

They started walking back toward the car.

"Thanks again," I called.

He nodded, raised a hand over his shoulder, but didn't look back. She took the keys from him and walked toward the driver's side. As he got into the car, she stopped and waved at me. For just a moment, I was jealous. Not of her so much, but of them, that they were traveling together. She checked her mirrors and pulled into traffic carefully.

I gunned Rosi's engine a couple of times to make sure that it was holding, checked the straps, and pulled on my helmet. I climbed on, kicked up the stand, and eased Rosinante into the first lane. A few miles down, I passed them like they were standing still, and in the rearview mirror, I saw them both wave.

Who knows, maybe Habibi and I aren't alone. Maybe there are couples like us everywhere, falling in love, living like it wasn't out of fashion. Maybe happy endings really do happen. I don't know. In any case, it was reason enough to keep going. I poured on a little more throttle and tucked in. "Almost home, Rosi," I said, and petted her tank.

No time

Beyond the hills, the sky got deep. The clouds all turned pastel and got pink, then a deep purple, and finally, they were blue silver and tucking into an easy night sky. The clock kept ticking on Rosinante's tank, playing bass to the frenetic tickity-tick-tack of her overheated engine. The engine block coughed smoke signals. She rested in a patch of gravel a few feet from me. Time had more than stopped. The last gas station I passed was closed, and with six useless dollars in my pocket, I ran her until she popped, sputtered, and lost compression entirely. There was still a slosh of gas in her, but she couldn't roll on any throttle. She wheezed when she idled, and for lack of a bullet, there was *nothing* I could do to finish her off. Rosinante would travel no further.

She was running on faith. If I didn't have it, she wouldn't go, and with only a few miles left to Habibi's front porch, she just quit. Not like forcing a safety stop, not even the slow creeping idle for the last twenty miles. She just quit. Almost like she knew something that I didn't. Maybe Habibi had already given up on me. Maybe she quit waiting, and Rosinante knew it.

Habibi hadn't answered a single phone call. She didn't call me, didn't try to find me, didn't come driving out to meet me in the final stretch. There were no secret commie messages attached to pink plastic roadside ribbon on any of the final fenceposts. No hidden bottles of whiskey, no instructions to lose my socks. There was *nothing*.

I laid down in the ditch, finishing my second to last cigarette, waiting for the last of the light to leave the sky, and for my inevitable midnight companion to arrive. My only companion outside of Rosinante. "Come on, Cap'n. Show yourself."

A slight breeze kicked up, rolling across the Columbia River, tangling in the tall grass down by the banks, building to a dying desert wind across the highway, to deposit him invisibly beside me.

Rosinante makes a gorgeous headstone.

As sad as it was, I was glad to hear his voice again, even if it was, in fact, my own. In the darkness, we make monsters, simply to pretend we are not alone. "I'm not done yet."

He laughed like it was an inside joke I missed. *Six weeks I'm gone and only to find you still here.*

"Maybe it's you that didn't move."

Ain't that the fuckin' truth. Hey, this place reeks. Seriously, you should be worried about mold spores or something. The corner is a stack of empty beer cans, the basement stairs look like twelve steps to an ashtray. And you, you look like shit, man.

"Am I dead?"

Not quite.

"I was just wondering if this is heaven." I stretched out again and knit my fingers behind my head. "I hope this is heaven, because this place rocks."

You're lying in a ditch. Here, it's beside the highway. There, it's a shithole basement. Either way, you're not in great shape.

"Yeah, lying in a ditch next to a busted-ass motorcycle. I have a backpack for a pillow, a leather jacket for a blanket, and a hallucination for a friend. By all rights, this should suck."

It does.

"But it doesn't."

You've lost the plot.

"No, Cap'n. I think finally figured it out." I sat up and found my last cigarette. "This is exactly where I wanted to be. I chose this. Every last minute of it: the fear, the desperation, the quest. I wanted this and so I made it happen. I got everything I wanted and so I have to assume that this is heaven."

What about your Habibi?

I smiled. "She's close."

I told you, she left you. She doesn't want you. She doesn't want a drunk for a boyfriend.

"But she's here, Cap'n."

She's gone.

"No, Cap'n. She's here, she's been here all along. She's watching us now."

You should know that your roommates are worried about you. You fell through one of the front hedges, last night. Man was that ever a laugh.

"Take me there."

You really wanna go home?

"Yeah. Take me home."

Your choice, buddy.

I watched him move, a bleak impression of a figure. He was translucent, a body rising from the asphalt. He was no more than a shadow, but hanging in midair, cast against *nothing* and standing before me. We stood facing each other. *You know that when you get there, she won't be there.*

"I know."

And you're ready for this?

I smiled my submission. "I'm ready."

The shadow shrugged. *You know this is the end, then.*

"Can't fight the future, can I?"

He laughed. The world behind him wavered, but it was all fiction anyway. *You can, and you have, but it was all for nothing.*

I laughed back. "It always was."

He nodded. *Alright. Let's get it over with.* He stepped back. The dark swirled, spiraled, and expanded around him. My shadow spread, and as it did, it ruffled like wings at the edges. *Nothing* opened into a dark space. He raised his arms, spreading himself thin like black watercolors over a pastoral evening scene.

Go home, he said.

Boom

My left leg slept, hanging over the edge of the bed. The foot planted on the wet floor was numb. My beard itched. I scratched my chin and found a few weeks' growth. My skin was cold and clammy. My hair was wet. My hoodie was damp and smelled of wet cotton. My leather jacket lay half-draped over me, and the shoulders were wet. I laid there for a while, listening to the rain. And then I smelled the damp in everything, felt the ceiling pressing in, and opened my eyes to footsteps on the floorboards above my head. I had to shut them again, and then there was *nothing* again, and I floated in it.

When the bodies stopped moving, the house was still enough to hear the wind through the rhododendron bushes and the ticking of Rosinante's clock, under piles of paper and empty cigarette boxes, stacks of beer cans, and candle wicks sputtering low behind their saints. I found the clock half crammed into a shoebox of photographs and bottle caps buried beside the bed.

And she was there. She was hairpins on the milk crate next to the bed, countless water glasses and twigs tied together in pink roadside plastic ribbon. She was a few swigs left in a bottle of my favorite whiskey, found next to a fencepost in West Richland, attached to a note that read: "lose your socks." She was piles of scribbled notebook pages strewn across my desk, abandoned drafts thrown in a milk crate in the corner, every note and scrap of paper she'd ever left for me. She was there in everything. But she wasn't there. Hadn't been there in weeks, or maybe months.

The front door opened upstairs.

I clawed at the back of the clock, but I couldn't get it open. The hands were frozen, the plastic casing was cracked and stippled in baked-on duct-tape adhesive, the face was blotted out in black scribbles, but the motor still made a faint ticking sound, counting down the hours left in the battery. Now there was no time, just a lonely but intrepid ticking. Shadows danced against the walls to the bomb-like rhythm of a heart left buried, beating, and waiting.

A set of keys hit the coffee table. A body hit the couch. I glanced at the digital alarm clock hanging from the ceiling above my bed. It was almost three in the morning. I figured Randy was home.

Swaying through my stale drunk, I tried to stand. The dead leg gave out and I fell against my shelves. I leaned and staggered, getting closer to the desk, clawing at stacks of paper, tossing empty beer cans. The leg came back in hard tingles, and I kicked it against the floor until I could feel it come to life again.

I stumbled up the stairs, still fumbling at the back of the clock.

Randy sat on the couch, watching TV with the volume low, and looking through the mail.

"Hey, Aaron."

"Hey, Randy."

I sat down next to him and kept working at the clock. He watched me closely, like any minute I might do something stupid. "How's it going?"

"Alright." I shrugged.

"You finish the novel?"

I nodded. "Almost."

"How does it end?"

I stopped playing with the clock and took a few deep breaths, mostly to steady the spins. In a few minutes I had gone from a doomed run up the coast to haunting a flooded basement, it was a lot to process half drunk and cross eyed.

I held a hand over one eye, glanced over the coffee table, and for lack of a better blunt instrument, set the clock face down on the floor, and stomped on the back of the battery casing a few times. I smiled at Randy.

He leaned back, only smiling for my sake.

"Boom," I said.

He shrugged and nodded.

I picked up the clock and pried the battery out of the back.

Randy glanced past me to the door. Lue was out there, smoking a cigarette. Her eyes were wide. She opened the door. "That's not another one of our clocks, is it?"

"I think it's his," Randy said.

I nodded.

"About time," Lue said.

"Seriously," I said.

"How does it end, though?"

I glanced around. "It ends like this." I showed him the clock.

"What, breaking a clock?"

"Dead now," I said.

"So that's it?" Randy asked.

I nodded. "Boom."

"Now what?" he asked.

"Fuck if I know, man. Maybe I'll join AA, take up macramé."

"There's whiskey in the cupboard," Lue said.

"Yeah. That sounds good, too."

Epilogue: Wildflower

My ride was a redhead in a big, brown family wagon van. Her name was Zoe, and the huge, lumbering monstrosity is what she called her "Piemobile." The seats were plush, and I was told that the benches in back folded out into a bed. She was playing old hip-hop cassettes on the tape deck and smoking a blunt. She was only nineteen. Until yesterday, she washed dishes at the restaurant. This morning, we picked up our paychecks, cashed them, and collected gifts from the rest of the crew. Zack and Kara brought her two pies and me a bottle of whiskey.

She was headed to San Francisco, and I was just headed south. It wasn't much of a plan, but we had a few weeks to figure out the rest. She had two ounces of chronic with her, a strain she called "The Ghost." On the way out of the city, we smoked two blunts on the roof of her dealer's apartment and rolled a few more. I was already stupid stoned, and she just kept on puffing. The Ghost was thoroughly fucking with my ability to navigate, and I had one stop left to make. "Get off here." I pointed at the exit.

She groomed the ash from the end of her blunt and eased the van off the freeway. "Where are we going again?"

"It's just a few miles off the freeway." The exit veered right onto a street shaded in tall trees. I checked the map and watched the signs. The sun mottled the street ahead with a sort of deceptive cheer.

Despite the fact that it had rained for months, we picked the first sunny day in spring to get rolling. We turned onto a narrow, two-lane stretch. A golf course opened up behind the trees and spread in rolling green to our right. A tall thicket of forest and bushes loomed at our left. "I think this is the spot," I said. "Let's see if we can turn around somewhere up ahead." The first wide patch Zoe found, she turned the Piemobile around and eased it off onto the thin shoulder.

"You think the po-po is going to be around?" She took a long pull from the blunt and eyed the few inches left.

"Not when you need them." I dug behind the seat and found only one grocery bag. "What happened to the other one?"

"I threw some of your stuff in back." She passed me the blunt again. Damn Ghost.

We climbed out and stretched like we'd already been driving for a few hours instead of the twenty-minute ride from the restaurant. Sarah was right about the place, though, there was something dark about it. I thought about telling Zoe to stay where she was, but it was too late. She was standing behind the van, puffing on her blunt and pulling her arms out of her sweatshirt sleeves. "It's a fuckin' nice day, Cap'n." She opened the back door and set her blunt on the bumper. She'd be fine.

"Grab that other bag while you're back there." I walked across the ditch and climbed up the embankment on the other side.

She pulled off her hoodie and tossed it in the back of the van. "What are those things?"

"Seeds," I told her.

"A lot of them." She opened the grocery bag and peered in. "What is this place?"

I glanced back into the woods. Behind the thicket of blackberries and ferns, a thin layer of underbrush veiled piles of trash and old tires. A soiled blanket grew up between the strata. It was the sight of clothes that made me shudder. "It's a bad place," I said. No use worrying her with the ghost story until we were a few miles away. I took a big handful of the seeds and pitched them back into the woods. "But it's gonna be a fuckin' flower garden when I get done with it."

"*Slovo,*" she said.

"Word," I said.

"See, yer gittin it," she said. She took a pull from her blunt. "Is this illegal?"

I glanced back into the dumping ground and down the road to either side. "Probably, but then again, it's entirely necessary." I flung handfuls down the embankment, trying to keep the seeds in the sunny areas. The ground was still wet enough that they should take pretty easily.

Zoe stood beside the ditch watching me. When I looked up at her, she offered me the blunt. "So, you're planting flowers?" she asked. Apparently, The Ghost was getting to her as well.

I shook another handful out and took the blunt from her. "*We're* planting flowers, yer Pieness."

She smiled wide and stony. "How delightfully pie of us," she quipped. She reached into the bag and pulled out a handful, tossing them around the ditch lazily.

We burned the blunt to a roach and emptied both the bags over a hundred yards of embankment and ditch. The way I had it figured, if even a tenth of those seeds sprouted, the dark and looming forest would be lost behind a wall of daisies, daffodils, sunflowers, and whatever else was in the bags. Lue collected them for weeks. Her parting gift was a Mapquest page and all the wildflower seed packets she could scrounge. It seemed a fitting collection for an exorcism. As Zoe got back into the van, I said a brief prayer.

"Where to next, Cap'n?" she asked as I climbed in.

I cracked the cap on the whiskey and took a long pull, sputtering approval. "You ever met an Amazon before?" I asked.

"Not that I know of." Zoe frowned.

"I think you'll like them." I took another long swig.

"Do the Amazons like pie?" she asked.

"Indeed they do. They love pie."

"I think we'll get along just fine then."

She started the van and flipped through the cassettes. When she found the one she was looking for, she popped it into the tape deck. The speakers thumped instantly.

"What is this?" I asked.

"Public Enemy. 'It Takes a Nation of Millions to Hold Us Back.'"

I smiled. I guess I might have chosen a nice, lonely steel guitar to play us out of town, something slow and outlawish, but I guess it worked.

"*Poyehali,*" she said.

"Indeed," I said. "let's roll."

She dropped the Piemobile into gear and pulled back onto the street. "Thirteen- hundred miles." I said, petting the dashboard.

Acknowledgements:

It's been a long process, and I owe a lot of beer and gas money to a lot of different people. Most of you probably know who you are and a few of you might even be keeping score. But just in case you don't, or you aren't, I have compiled a small list. Mostly so that if you ask me if you're in the novel, I can say yes. I don't think anybody actually reads the acknowledgements, so if you find your name in here, please feel free to redeem the free beer coupon. In no particular order: Habibi, and the family. (.) Randy "Conduit" Etherton, Luara, Jordan, Gabe, Conlon, Crystal, Rusty and the whole Stronghold crew as well as the extended family. Thanks for taking me in when I was homeless. Sorry about the busted clocks and pissing in your flower bed. Airola, my distant Jedi techie, I owe you pitchers. Aaron Howard, for being my first random fan, and the Silent Buzz, yes you Alan, for asking me for my autograph. All of the Arson Island crew, the Treehuggers, and the Mach12e cogs. (Eat a bag of dicks.) The Flight to Mars people, if you can call them that. Blake, and all of the lost boys. Hope you get to read this someday. Kaz, I miss you man. Fuck em if they can't take a joke. You would have loved this one. Tab, Jeff, Fitz, Danny, Joe, (you try flingin' pizzas after four of those damn cocktails), as well as all my friends at the Daley Double Saloon. Sorry, too many to list, and the names get fuzzy after a few drinks. (kisses Francine and Marianne). Scott, Alejandro, Cesar, Fredy, Cain, both Katies, Sarah, the BZs, Austin, Lisa and Jimmy Joe, His Highness Scottito and his family, Teresita, Sheba, every customer that is or ever was a part of the 101 Diner. Dennis, Peanut "nutbiter" the poodle. Hot damn, this is getting out of control. Hell, it's my book, I do what I want. The Amazons, of course, especially my RittyK and Lara, yes, they're still intact. I still got yo key. Sue and Dallas for both introducing me to the craft, and helping me refine it, irrespectively. Thanks for your patience. Scritches behind all appropriate ears. Elijah, I have made a space for it in my bookshelf. I am ready for it to be real. Bewah, it's done, damnit. Quit bugging me. Mat Zabas, for making the ink in my blood very real, for helping me fix every ugly rusted out street nag I've ever brought to your immaculate chop shop, and for doing a great job of playing cynic. Yer still an asshole. Qathi for selling me her ratbike and offering her support through the process, for amazing shots, and a mach-yes attitude. Tell JB to roll over damnit. She's snoring. Michele Lee McMullen for picking up the pieces and putting it together so that somebody would actually get to read it. I owe my eternal gratitude to my editors, for doing the unpaid, and seemingly thankless job of cleaning up my mess: Teresa "Queen of the Harpies" Stanker, for bleeding it, and Larry "Doc Jernigan" Wampler, for bandaging it back up. Of course, Mom and Pop, for raising me to be a consummate dreamer and a man with a talent for doing what needs to get done, respectively. And last, but certainly not least, my delicious squishy, Caro-la Reyna. For her incredible patience throughout the process, and for making sure that I eat something once in a while. I'm done, squishface. I'll be in bed soon. "*Ya. No mas.*"

(The secret track.)

Of Broads and Bears

Once upon a time, there was a little girl named Goldilocks. One day, while walking through the woods she came to a little house. She walked right in and made herself at home. She tried every bowl of porridge until she found the one that was just right. Then she tried every chair until she found the one that was just right. Then she tried every bed until she found the one that was just right. Then she went home and told all of her little blonde friends about it. The next thing you know, there's a couple boutiques, the prices went way up, and it was nearly impossible to find any parking anywhere in Beartown.

After a few months, Goldilocks Inc. decided that the whole of Beartown was indeed just right. They bought all the land out from under the bears, leveled the houses and a good deal of the forest, and turned the whole place into a trendy little mall with a rustic feel and hundreds of little bistros that served Thai fusion and expensive Italian and that sort of thing. There were three Starbucks in the place, you know what I mean? So the bears either worked for the tourists or they shit in the woods.

One day, a guy came along that sold animatronic forest animals, so most of the real forest animals were laid off and replaced with robot animals that did seem life-like, and never shit anywhere.

A few of the real forest animals got into wildlife relocation programs, and got sent out to national parks. A few animals got gigs with petting zoos. The rest just sort of wandered off.

The last time I saw a real bear he was sitting next to a freeway offramp in a soiled flannel shirt, with a sign that read: "Will gobble you up for food."

I gave him some change and a couple cigarettes, but never made eye contact.

Made in the USA
Charleston, SC
21 January 2014